When We Wake

When We Wake

K. Lee

Charleston, SC
www.PalmettoPublishing.com

First Edition

Hardcover ISBN: 978-1-63837-850-1
Paperback ISBN: 978-1-63837-849-5
eBook ISBN: 978-1-63837-848-8

To the person who gave me the strength to put myself first.

-K-

Prologue

Two children are running in Central Park. Their laughter echoes as they climb on rocks without a care in the world. There are no parents, no teachers, no one to yell or scream or fuss. There is only ever laughter. For the girl and the boy have met in a dream only they know of.

The girl, only six but so fierce. She isn't afraid of anything because every morning she wakes up to a nightmare— parents who sniff white powder that makes them happy and forgetful. She is only seen in her dreams.

The boy, seven but very curious. His life consists of eight-bedroom houses and indoor swimming pools. He has never known a life of poverty or parents who don't want him. He knows of parents who ask too much of him, who ask him to be perfect.

The boy gets a lead on the girl, pushing her as he goes by. He laughs as the sweat rolls down his face. He can hear his heart beating in his chest. The best part of dreaming is that you can make anything happen. He closes his eyes and with all his might leaps into the air. He lands on the nearest tree branch, feeling stronger than he ever has.

"Yes!" He laughs. "I beat you! I'm the bestest!"

The boy looks around to gloat, but the girl is nowhere to be seen. He thinks she disappeared, but then he hears her voice behind him. "Boo!" she yells. He loses his balance, falling from the tree, and as he falls, he thinks of the only thing that can save him. He lands on the softest mattress he could dream of.

In the tree, the girl starts to laugh. "You thought you won, but I was up here waiting for you."

"That's not fair! You scared me!" the boy complains, his London accent stronger than ever.

The girl sighs and rolls her green eyes. She jumps. As she's free-falling, all the boy can think is how fearless she is. Her blue dress—making her red hair even more enticing—puffs up like an upside-down teacup, helping her fall gracefully. It reminds him of *Alice in Wonderland*. He looks away so he doesn't see under her dress. His mother always tells him to be a gentleman.

When the girl sticks the landing, the mattress sags and knocks him over. He stays down, looking up at her.

"Do you think you're real?" he asks.

"Of course I'm real! Aren't you?"

"Well, if you're real, and I'm real, one of us is dreaming."

The girl sighs and sits, wrapping her arms around her knees. "I was hoping you wouldn't say that. I knew we were. I just wanted to be happy for a little while."

"You're not happy? Do you not get a lot of toys?" He wonders what it would be like to never have the best toys to bring to show-and-tell on Monday mornings.

"I wish that was it." The girl sighs again and lies down next to him, staring into his hazel eyes. "My parents are sick, I think. They are always dizzy and don't work a lot. Sometimes I hear them throwing up late at night. I'm not supposed to get out of bed, I know, but I can't help it. I don't think they remember me some days. They won't go to a doctor either."

"Wow—my parents are never home! They're always working to make more money for my toys. I have so many toys. I wish I could show you them."

The girl pouts for a moment, her eyes sad. Then they brighten as she has an idea. "Maybe you could think of them and bring them here! You've already thought of a mattress. Try it!"

The boy closes his eyes and gives it a minute's thought before he finds the perfect toy for them both to play with. When he opens his eyes, there's a giant teddy bear on a nearby rock just waiting to be climbed on.

The little girl squeals and claps her hands. She pushes him down to give herself a head start, giggling the whole way. The boy smiles and jogs after her, letting her win. He won the first time; he should let her win once. When she's close enough, the girl leaps and tackles the bear.

As she plays, the boy sits down to watch. He feels sick inside, like something is crawling around in his stomach whenever she smiles. His face even gets hot when she looks at him too long. He doesn't know what he's feeling; he just knows he doesn't want to wake up.

When the girl calms down a bit, she invites him to join her. He tackles the giant teddy bear, knocking it on its back and taking them with it. They laugh and giggle for what seems like hours. Everything seems so slow, but the time passes too fast.

Suddenly, everything starts to shift as reality pull them toward their beds. The boy can feel his body being shaken by the maid. The girl can hear her parents yelling in the middle of the night. The girl sighs. "I guess this is it. I have to go now. This dream has been my favorite. Thanks for the teddy bear."

"Well, I did get it for me..." the boy jokes.

The girl giggles as she walks away into the trees.

"Wait!" the boy yells. When she hears him, she holds on, fighting waking up, and he calls, "What's your name?"

She smiles. "Eleanor. What's yours?"

"Eli!"

"It was nice to meet you, Eli!" Eleanor yells back as she's pulled back to her shivering body curled up next to a space heater. She can hear her parents more clearly now. For once, she stays in her bed and prays to a God she doesn't believe in, that they'll stop so she can go back to sleep and see the boy of her dreams.

Eleanor

Present Day

My first reaction when I see him is to run. He looks *so* handsome. That's a three-thousand-dollar suit, I'm sure; he would never wear anything else. The cafe outside of my hotel is partially a bookstore, and he's reading something at the corner table with his sunglasses on. I barely recognize him at first. I tell myself I'm seeing things, or maybe even dreaming after all this time, so I pinch myself to make sure it's real.

I try to hide from him while I look him over. His suit is dark navy—it almost looks black.

His tie looks loose like he couldn't breathe having it too tight. His leg is shaking nervously and I can see that he hasn't eaten the food that he ordered. The ice coffee in front of him has little to no ice left. I wonder how long he's been here.

As I rub the skin on my arm, I walk over to him slowly, hoping he won't shy away. He makes time stop; everyone in the room is gone and it's just me and him like old times. Whatever he's reading absorbs him, because even when I'm standing right in front of him, he doesn't notice. I almost think he's ignoring me. I might as well say hello. I cough. "Eli," I say shakily, "is that really you?"

Eli smiles and puts his book down. He takes off his sunglasses, and the sun beams directly into his beautiful eyes. "El, I thought that was you walking in. Wow you haven't changed at all."

I suck in a gulp of air, relieved that he hasn't changed either. Eli, the boy of my dreams—quite literally—is sitting in a cafe in Dalston, London, and he still remembers me.

1

"I, um, thought I was dreaming again," I say. "I even had to pinch myself."

This makes Eli laugh out loud. His laugh echoes through the cafe. "Isn't it too early for you to be up? New Yorkers usually take longer to get over their jet lag."

"Well, yes, I've already been here a few days and—wait, how did you know I would be here?" We could dream with each other, but seeing the future was a whole new ball game.

"I read it, actually. Saw it in some newspaper. Some chap here was reading, and I paid him to give it to me. Your name was on the front page." My cheeks warm as Eli stares at me and adds, "I didn't think I'd see you here. I'd planned on coming to your first book signing… I had to find out if you were real."

"Of course I'm real," I say, smiling. My heart is pounding out of my chest. I can hear it in my ears. How is it possible we end up at the same exact café? "You're the one that isn't real."

"Oh, so you think you're still dreaming, huh?"

I laugh. "I mean, kind of."

I never thought we would see each other again after our last dream. We told each other it wouldn't be the last, but we both knew it was. Was I dreaming right now? Did I make it to the hotel, fallen asleep? This isn't normal for us to be able to dream together. After all these years, we could never get back to where we had always met. Eli makes a face at me and says, "How have you been?"

The first thing I can think of is to tell him my parents are dead.

"I've been OK…" I hesitate to tell him what's happened since he's been gone. I've always been so closed off. Would telling him make things worse or better? "My parents died."

"Oh, I'm so sorry, love."

"Eh… don't be." I sigh and wave off his apology. Hearing him call me love again takes my breath away. "It was years ago."

"Really? That's something, at least." Eli can find the light at the end of any tunnel. "I hope I don't die sober. What a terrible way to live."

I laugh. "Well, you're not an alcoholic, are you?"

"No, of course not. I'm just a really big fan of it."

I laugh again, feeling my heart in my throat. I don't know how it's so hard to talk to him; it's *Eli*. He's perfect. He always made me feel wanted, even on my darkest days, or rather, my parents' darkest days. He was my sweetest friend. And as far as I knew, he was just a dream in my head, a place to go when I was upset.

"Do you have plans?" Eli asks. He looks excited, like he's been planning this for years. "Could I show you around town?"

My heart aches in my chest making it hard to breathe. I can feel my face getting red, so flustered from trying to process that Eli is even here. I could be dreaming right now but wouldn't I know? My mind is telling me that I should say no but my heart wants to see what would happen if I said yes.

"Sure," I say coolly.

He stands and shows me to the door. He even opens it for me. He always said his mother taught him to be a gentleman. There's a man out front with a jet-black town car waiting with a door open for Eli. He waves off his driver, who winks at me before getting in the driver's seat and taking off. To say I'm impressed is an understatement.

"The driver is someone who works for my father, but he didn't need him today." He says his eyes swimming with bitterness. "You're probably wondering why I'm here, right?"

I smile and nod at his question, loving that he can still read my mind.

"Right," he says. "Well, over time, I started to hate sleeping. It was a long time coming. That cafe is open twenty-four hours a day, did you know? So I would walk there every night for a good read and some coffee."

I listen to him talk.

"Yes, well, my parents left me everything since my father 'retired.' He still teaches at the hospital—he taught me, you know. The medical practice all kind of fell in my lap, and I didn't know how to handle it at first. Didn't think I was ready yet, but my father sure did. He would say, 'Son of mine, it's just like when I taught you to swim. What did I do? Throw you in.' So he threw me in, I guess."

"Wow, that's—wow."

It's baffling how easily he talks to me. I know eventually he will ask me how I'm doing, and I don't have an answer. That's the reason I'm in London in the first place. Too much of my life has been dictated by someone else; even now, when I'm a successful woman in my career, I still don't feel like myself.

After my folks died, I took a look at my life and realized how unhappy I was. When I first met Eli, I felt like a million bucks even when I woke up. I haven't felt that way since I was seventeen years old. I'm thirty-five now. Seeing him again after all this time makes me feel things I never felt when I was a child.

Just like that, Eli interrupts my thoughts, making my heart flutter by asking, "What about you?"

Eli

Present Day

As she talks, I can't help but stare at her lips. She was my first kiss, and I always wanted her to be my last. I never could bring myself to love anyone the way I loved her. She's the only girl I've ever truly loved. But she doesn't know it, and I want to keep it that way.

Eleanor is walking next to me. *This is real life*, I keep telling myself. She's really here. I have to keep myself from getting too excited; I'm waiting for the other shoe to drop. She's going to slip away from me. Just like every other time. Her hair is still as red as ever. I want to run my fingers through it.

After all this time with no contact I can't believe she's here. The last time I tried to contact Eleanor was through email over ten years ago. It was crushing finding out that she was never going to respond, that I was left to figure out who I was without her. She broke my heart.

When I first found out she would be coming to England, I imagined all the things I could do to meet up with her. Picking her up at the airport, finding what hotel she was staying at and find her there… I was terrified that I was going to scare her off or ambush her.

Now I can't believe she's talking to me, listening to me talk about my life thus far. Not only did I not get to dream with her anymore, emailing stopped too. That was sparce enough, for her to cut me off completely was heart wrenching. I felt like a drug addict going cold turkey; I had no way of getting my fix.

Over all my years of knowing El, she was never shy. She made me feel more alive. Everything she did, she did with such courage. Granted, it was only a dream; anything was possible there. Maybe she really isn't the girl I loved. Maybe that girl only exists in my dreams.

"And that's why I only just got here," El says, interrupting my thoughts. "I thought maybe I'd see you, but after all these years…I told myself I'd made it up."

I laugh. "You and me both, kid." She always hated when I called her *kid.* Just because I was less than a year older than her, I got to call her a kid. "I saw a therapist for a while too."

"Really?" she asks, and when I nod, she adds, "I didn't think that you would need a therapist."

"Well, I didn't. I thought I was fine, but my parents said I was depressed, so…therapy it was. Either that or I had to tell them what was wrong."

"Which no one will ever believe."

"Exactly." I chuckle. "You were the only one who ever got that, and you lived on the opposite side of the world."

"Well, not complete opposite. Separate countries, same ocean."

"Ah, yes. Sorry to mix that up, love."

Her face gets red, and I can tell she's feeling mixed emotions every time I call her "love." It's an old habit. For a long time, she was my only one. Eventually, I started calling all girls that.

"So where to now?" she asks. "I'd like to think you've planned this out. Since you knew I was coming."

I smile at her. "I had a few ideas if things worked out... Follow me."

Eleanor

Age 11

All I wanted to do was go to sleep. I knew Eli was waiting for me. We were supposed to go swimming in the giant pool he'd dreamed of the night before. I'd never been swimming; I'd never even been to a pool to learn how. That was what Eli was going to show me. I was *so* late.

"Do you even care what happens to me and your mother?" my dad shouted at me. "Why do you think you're so damn special? Because you're smart?"

I had gotten an A on a paper for the first time in my life, and I had made the mistake of telling my parents about it before bed. All the times I tried to get good grades and make sure I didn't miss school was for *them*. I wanted them to be proud of me. To look at me like I mattered to them, like I wasn't just some wasted mistake they didn't have room for. They only saw me as a punching bag for whenever they needed to let out some anger.

My dad was so close to my face I could smell the different alcohols on his breath. It was mostly beer, but I could also smell some hard liquor. Vodka. Being only eleven, I shouldn't have known these things, but it was normal for me. If I had mentioned to one of my peers at school that I knew what kind of alcohol my parents had for breakfast, they would've thought I was crazy.

"You know, you don't come from a line of smart people, so I don't know how you're gettin' those kinda grades," my mom slurred. "You must be cheatin'.'"

"If there's one thing worse than a stupid child, it's a cheater." My dad wound up his fist and hit me on the side of my head. My ears rang, and for a second I thought I even blacked out. This had happened so many times that I just braced myself for it. Lying on the ground, I could hear my parents' faint laughter. The pain radiated all through my skull. It felt like a sledgehammer hitting me over and over. Maybe my dad was doing just that.

I'm not a cheater, I tried to say. The words couldn't form; my brain felt like scrambled eggs. My legs were jelly. My arms covered my head after the first blow, taking the brunt of the beating. I would probably struggle to write a simple sentence in school after this.

When the continuous pounding and spitting finished, they finally retired to the couch. I waited to move; for a while, I couldn't have even if I wanted to. Paralyzed with fear, I didn't really know what would happen if I tried while they were still awake.

Sitting up was hard. Once I finally did, a pain started in my neck and ran down my back. I knew I would be bruised all over my body. I couldn't go swimming *now*.

Unfortunately, in our dream world I couldn't cover up my scars and bruises. I'd tried every time me and Eli dreamed together, but I was never able to. I was embarrassed by my ugly body. I felt like every time Eli looked at me, he thought I was ugly. Plus, Eli didn't get how much it bothered me to talk about my parents. They embarrassed me too.

My bed was still a little kid's bed. It was a pink race car that my grandma had given to my mom before I was born. They hadn't bothered to get me a new one, and now that I was starting to outgrow it, it was hard for me to sleep on it. Some nights, I woke up on the ground. It was probably why I woke up more often than Eli did. It didn't stop me from seeing him, though.

I loved being around Eli. He made me feel so special, even right after my parents disciplined me. There had never been a time when I'd rather be awake than dreaming with him. My mind played over some of our recent times together. None of them involved bruises. Mom and

Dad had been OK until tonight, which had been my fault anyway. I'd *known* I shouldn't bother them.

With the pain in my head and all over my body, it didn't take long to fall asleep. Eli was waiting for me with his feet dipped in a gigantic pool. It was shaped like a lightning bolt, the zigzags making it look like a perfect place to race.

I looked down at myself. Of course, I was already wearing a bathing suit. I had bruises on my ribs and lower stomach and a few on my face. There were even some on my forearms. I knew I couldn't go swimming now. There was no way I'd let Eli see me like this. It was too much even for me. Tearing up, I noticed that he hadn't seen me yet. I imagined myself wearing anything else. When I looked down again, Iwas wearing a tank top over my bathing suit. That could work.

Walking up to Eli, I cleared my throat. "Can I wear this in the pool?" I asked. "I don't really wanna show my whole body."

He smiled up at me. "Sure, El. Whatever you want." He got up to give me a hug. I winced in pain but tried my best to hide it. "Ready?"

I did my best to smile and nod, feeling my skin throbbing. Eli jumped in first, holding his legs to his chest, making a huge splash that soaked me.

"It's called a cannonball," he said. "Now you have to jump in, and I'm going to catch you."

Fear crept up my back. What if I drowned? I would wake up and be home again. I'd just got here. Our dreamworld was the only place I wanted to be. This was my home—Eli was. There wasn't a reason to fear him catching me. I knew he would. There was no doubt about it.

"I got you, El. Don't worry."

That was the first time I ever trusted Eli completely. Jumping into a vast, endless pool was the first time Eli saw me willing to be vulnerable. We were only eleven, but there was so much going on in our lives. The only people we wanted to trust were each other. That dream helped me figure that out. It was a dream I would never forget. They all were.

Eli

Age 13

My foot tapped the floor, impatient, waiting for my mother to come out of the home office with my dad. Getting sent home from school had never been my ideal day, but today I had wanted to be sent home. Eleanor was turning thirteen, the same age as me. We were only the same age for a few months every year, and I wanted to see her sooner rather than later.

I had stopped telling my parents about El when I was eight; for my birthday, I'd wanted to fly to New York to meet her, and they thought I was crazy to think I would be allowed to meet a stranger that lived over seas. I told them she was a pen pal. So she stayed in my dreams. It wasn't every dream, and it wasn't every night, but it was often enough.

My dad came out of his office first, his face red with anger. "You do not get sent home from school. You do not start fights with other kids. You do not piss off your father when he's in the middle of a goddamn surgery!"

"Henry!" my mom exclaimed. "I think you've said enough."

"No, Claire, I don't think I have. Our son has *never* done something like this in his life. He's better than this. He's an embarrassment to our family name."

"I'm right here, you know," I said firmly, "and I don't care what you think, Father."

"Well, you should." His voice echoed through the living room. "Until you've figured out what our family name should mean to you, you can go to your room."

That was all I wanted. I didn't say a word as I stood up and headed to my bedroom. My room was on the third floor of our three-story
terrace. My parents never needed the big room, so they gave it to me
when I was born. They knew the nanny would need a bathroom for the
late nights when they weren't home or they just weren't in the mood to
pick me up. I got the master bedroom.

My parents never got me the way El did, or even my nanny, who
cared for me like I was her own son.

My nanny was the best. She did the parenting thing. She took me
to parks and the zoo. She picked me up from school when my parents forgot. She made me feel loved. So when I got in trouble—which
wasn't often—she was there for me. Though my parents never missed
football games or school events of any kind; they had to make sure that
we looked like the happy family everyone thought we were.

"Honey," Nanny June said. "You can't get yourself in trouble like that."

"I don't care," I said with my head on my pillow. It was already nine
o'clock where El lived; I just wanted to sleep. "Can I take a nap now?"

She came over to feel my forehead. "Thirteen-year-olds don't nap.
Are you sure you're OK?"

"I'm fine, June," I said, pushing her hand off my face. I turned over
so she wouldn't see my pained expression when I added, "Please go away."

Nanny June sighed. When I heard the door shut, my eyes shut as
well. It wasn't long before everything went completely dark, and I woke
to birds chirping and water sloshing against the bank.

Every time I woke up in my dreams, I was lying on the ground. Eleanor said she was always standing, but I lay on my back, looking up at
the sky, whether it was a cloudy night or a blue sky. I stood up, observ-
ing my surroundings. I thought I was in Crystal Palace Park. The lake
was surrounded by dinosaur sculptures. I remembered coming with
Nanny June when I was just a little boy.

"Where are we?" Eleanor whispered in my ear, startling me.

I whirled and saw her smiling at me. "Crystal Palace Park," I said
shakily. "I used to come here when I was younger."

"Oh, you and your fabulous life." El laughed. I could see just a faint bruise on her cheek. When I reached out to touch her, she shied away from my fingers.

"El, what happened?" I asked.

"Not on my birthday," she begged. There was an unforgettable sadness in her eyes. "Please."

She almost sounded desperate, so I let it go. I knew my parents had their issues, but I had never been wrongfully hit or spanked. Eleanor showed up with a new bruise or cut or scrape every time I dreamed with her. I hated her parents more than I hated mine.

"Fine," I said. "How does it feel to be the same age as me? Cool, huh?"

"You've been asking me that for as long as I can remember," El accused. "I still feel the same as I did when I was twelve."

"Yes, but you're a teenager now. It's going to be different."

"Why d'you talk like that? All proper and whatnot."

"I'm...British. It's kind of how we talk," I said. "Besides, my parents make me go to the best schools. So I have good English."

"Oh," she muttered. "OK."

"What?"

"Nothing."

"Tell me or I'll ask about that bruise again," I threatened.

El sighed and rolled her eyes at me the way she always did. "You're just better than me. That's all."

"Ha! Better than you? No one is better than you."

I blushed and so did she.

We were silent as we made our way through the park to the lake with the dinosaurs. I remembered almost falling off one of the sculptures. Nanny June let me wear flip-flops, which caused me to slip around.

All of a sudden, I remembered I was going to dream up some of her favorite food, with roses and candles. I'd seen it on the telly once and thought it would be romantic. I led her into the maze. I knew it forward and backward. She giggled and I let her make some wrong turns. When we made it to the middle—which took us longer than it would've taken me—I thought about our dinner. Eleanor saw it first: the cloth-covered table with a vase filled with roses and a silver platter with a lid.

"Is this for me, Eli? Really?"

"Of course, love," I said, matter-of-fact. "Who else would it be for?"

"Maybe the dinos," she joked, her cheeks still slightly pink.

When we got to the table, I helped seat her. In my head I was thinking this was a date. My first. I didn't even know how dates worked. My parents went on them all the time without me, but I certainly didn't know what I was doing. I couldn't help but wonder if she was thinking the same thing.

Once she was seated, I lifted the lid off the platter.

"Ravioli!" she exclaimed. "You remembered?"

"Of course," I said. "You've dreamed them up more times than I can count. These ones are going to be extra good."

She giggled.

After our meal, we climbed on the dinosaurs with our dreamed-up Nerf guns. Ours fired bullets, but it didn't matter. Every time we were shot in our dreams, we either woke up or healed ourselves. It depended where we got hit.

There was a carousel not far from the park, but I knew it would take a while to walk. El was a big fan of jumping, ever since our first dream together. So we raced just like old times. She beat me like always. Since I'd turned ten, I'd been able to outrun her, but I let her win. From the moment I met her, I *always* let her win. She deserved it. She deserved more than she knew.

The carousel was magical in real life and in my dreams. Riding it was endless; you never had to stop. Eleanor and I never did. We rode the carousel until we were dizzy, feeling as if we were going to throw up. We rode until we were being pulled apart once again, drifting away like a soul from its body when it's finally ready to let go of life. We would wake up to start another day pretending the other doesn't exist until we were able to see each other in our dreams once again.

Eleanor

Present Day

As Eli and I walk, I wonder where he's taking me. There's no doubt in my mind it will be somewhere special, most likely a place he's shown me before. All this time, I thought I was insane. I never thought in my wildest dreams—pun intended—that I would end up where I am. I didn't even think Eli was real; sometimes I still don't think he is.

"I can't believe you're really here," he says, grabbing my hand. His is warm but rough, like there's a secret behind them. "You have no idea how much I've missed you."

I snort. "You didn't even know if I was real or not."

"I always did when we still had contact," he retorts. "You're the one who didn't."

I pull my hand away and clasp it in the other. From the tone in his voice, I know he's exactly what he's talking about. I broke off all contact from him—emailing, dreaming, anything that could allow him to connect with me again. The coming conversation will ruin the entire day, and I know that if we continue down this path we'll go back to how it was before. Both of us alone, or at least, *I* would be alone again.

"Can we not do this right now?" I say. I used to beg Eli not to bring up my bruises and scrapes. Eventually, he stopped asking.

"Fine." He sighs. "Do you want to know where we're going?"

"Of course. I just figured you'd want to surprise me."

Eli just nods. We walk in silence the rest of the way, me hoping he'll say something first. As soon as we arrive, I know exactly where we are. "Crystal Palace Park," I say. "It's really here."

"Of course it is. It's not made up." He grabs my hand once again. "Do you remember when I brought you here? Your thirteenth birthday?"

"Yes," I say. "It doesn't look like it's changed at all."

"It hasn't much. I come here quite often to visit. Sometimes I even take naps."

"Hoping to see me, huh?"

"Exactly what I try to do."

My heart is aching. How can I do this? How can I pretend like what we have isn't there? There isn't a moment that goes by where I don't think of him, but he doesn't know my past the way he once did. It's been so long since we last saw each other. He has no idea what I've been through, what I'm hiding from him. I'm not in London alone. How can I tell him who's with me? He'll run for the hills the first chance he gets.

We find a park bench to sit on. I take my hand back as I sit down. Eli was always personal, even before we let things get complicated. There's just something about holding his hand that makes me feel like I'll slip back into the Dreamworld with him and forget the only person who matters to me now.

My phone dings inside my purse. I've been ignoring it since I ran into Eli. It's the real world. I don't want to face it right now.

"I thought about coming here," I say. "I researched where it was, actually."

"Oh, really? Now why would you want to do that?" Eli jokes. "You would only have found little ol' me, you know."

"I'm aware," I tell him. "That's why I chickened out and came to the cafe instead. I was too scared to find you sitting on a park bench in your three-thousand-dollar suit feeding pigeons or something."

He laughs so loud he scares some birds from the nearby bushes. Everything is so green in London. Of course, that's probably from all the rain. Even though it isn't raining now, the air feels moist.

"How do you know how much I spent on this suit? I'll have you know, I got this on sale."

"Oh yeah? For how much?" I challenge him.

"Well…it was about four thousand."

"Ha! That's in pounds, I take it?"

He nods, scratching the back of his neck in embarrassment.

"That's almost five thousand dollars in America!" I say. "That's more than I thought."

"Yes, well, it was still on sale."

"I don't even want to know how much it was regularly. I try to find every sale I can, but you can drop five thousand on a suit."

"Well, you're here now," Eli says. "To make real money."

"I was making real money before. I'm making *more* money by coming here, is all."

"Are we really going to talk about money or about the elephant in the room? Or more so, the park?"

My heart starts racing. He knows. He knows and he's been testing me, waiting for me to tell him. He has probably already been judging me in his head. My phone goes off again. Thinking maybe I can change the subject, I pull my phone out to read the texts there.

James:

I miss you.

Where are you

Please call.

I close my eyes, knowing I'm hiding him from Eli, knowing it's not right. How do you bring something like that up? The most important person in your life needs you, and the most important person from your dreams wants your attention.

"El?" Eli touches my arm to pull me from my trance. "You OK?"

"Um…yeah," I lie, locking my phone and shoving it into my pocket. "I'm great."

Eleanor

Age 28

*C*rap, crap, crap, I said to myself as I missed another subway. I was going to be late for work again. A job at a publishing house was something I'd never thought I could land, but after college I finally had what I deserved. Missing the subway again could jeopardize everything for me. I knew the next train would take ten minutes to get there, and that was ten minutes I didn't have. I turned to leave and ran right into a tree-sized person who knocked me and everything I had on me to the ground. The floor of a subway station—not only horrifying but unsanitary.

"Motherf—"

"Whoa. A girl like you shouldn't talk like that."

I looked up to see a beautiful man about my age standing over me, looking amused. His glasses framed his face perfectly, like a model from the ads on the subway walls. His jet-black hair was pulled back in a bun; he was perfect for New York City.

"Oh yeah? And how should a girl like me talk, then?" I asked sarcastically. "A girl who, by the way, you haven't bothered to help pick up her things."

He chuckled as he bent down to help me. I was practically done when another train came through. The guy grabbed my arm softly. "Listen," he said. "I'm sorry. I honestly am. I didn't mean to upset you or anything."

"Seriously, dude, don't even worry about it. I cannot miss this train." I pulled myself from his grasp and headed for the doors. He got on the train with me. We stood in a crowd of strangers. "What, are you following me now?"

"Uh…this *is* a subway, right?" he asked, smiling.

I blushed, feeling a bit of a douche. He'd apologized and I continued to feel bitter. Looking at him standing next to me, I saw he had freckles across his nose. I hadn't seen that on a man in a long time. He seemed to be taking me in as well, looking at all my odd features, I was sure.

"I—I'm sorry," I stuttered. "Obviously I'm having a bad day, and I really can't be late for work again or I'll be fired. I'm surprised I even got the job I have."

"Do you want me to come down there and tell them some jerk of a guy ran into you on purpose just to talk to a beautiful girl?"

I blushed even harder, and my heart started to skip. I hadn't been talked to like that, well, ever. No guy made such an effort to try to get my attention. It was always catcalls and whistles. "I—um…I don't think they'd excuse me for that. No matter how handsome you are." I'd never flirted before either.

He smiled and rubbed the back of his neck. "Well maybe I'll have to find out where you work anyway. So I can find a way to contact you."

"Why don't I just give you my name? Then you can look me up."

"Wow—you really trust me that much?"

I laughed. I was holding onto the pole so hard I thought I might rip it out from its screws. There was only one more stop until mine, and I wanted to see this guy again. It'd been so long since I'd seen the outside of my apartment walls for anything other than work. I didn't really have any friends; my life was too complicated, and I didn't think anyone would want to put up with that. This guy, though, he put up with my attitude only seconds after meeting me.

"I didn't say I trusted you, but—" I took a deep breath, "—you don't seem crazy or like a killer. I think that's my two deal-breakers."

He laughed again. The train doors opened, and I realized this was my stop. He got off with me, and I thought I might be in some trouble.

"OK, *now* you're following me," I joked, slightly hesitant.

"Well, I had ten more blocks, but I need your name," he said, smiling.

"Eleanor. Eleanor Scott."

We were standing near the steps, and all of a sudden I was aware of where I was and how late I would be if I didn't run up the steps right then and there.

"OK, I *really* have to run." I started speed-walking up the stairs and then—"Wait, what's your name?"

He looked at me like he was taking me in again—maybe one last look. I did the same, and as I did, I felt so *good* about myself. It had been such a long time since I had talked to someone—other than my pets—about something besides horrible books or addiction. I'd just had a slightly normal conversation with a complete stranger, and it felt so good. So as he looked at me, I looked back at the frame of his glasses and where his lips turned up in a smile.

Until he said, "James. My name is James."

I grinned brightly. It was all I needed to return to the real world. "It was nice to meet you!" I shouted as I ran off. I heard him laugh.

The people I passed on the street were a blur. Even if I hadn't been in a rush, they would be blurry. I felt like I was back in my dream world—anything was possible. Waiting at a crosswalk, I spotted a man in a pair of blue scrubs. My heart sank, my dream world turning into a nightmare.

Eli

Age 29

Kit scowled at me. It was three in the bloody morning, and I was scheduled to work in two hours. She had just shaken me awake and turned on her bedside lamp. There was no way I'd fall back asleep; she knew what a light sleeper I was. She took advantage of that at times. This time, it wasn't pleasant.

"Who the hell is Eleanor?" she demanded again.

"What are you on about? Who?" I mumbled, taken off guard. Of course I knew who Eleanor was. She was my first love. She was the girl of my dreams. I kept it that way.

Some nights, I searched for her. I thought of her favorite places and tried to find her there. Kit didn't know about her. I'd only told one person about her since she'd left me, and I didn't think he believed me.

"Really? You seem to dream about this girl quite often," Kit said sharply. "She's all you seem to talk about when you sleep."

"Kit, really? I'm dreaming. Why are you reading so much into this?" I tried to wrap my arms around her waist, but she slipped away from me.

"Shouldn't I be, though? There was always something off with you. You've always seemed to have some secret, like something isn't being said. And now I know what it is. You're pining after some other woman who broke your heart." She got out of bed, her silky blush-pink nightgown barely covering her thighs. She had such nice, tan legs. They were one of my favorite features, and she knew it. I made sure she knew. The duvet I was tangled up in was making me hot, even though I only had trousers on. I ripped it off and followed Kit into the kitchen, where she was making a pot of tea. Which meant this was going to be a very long morning.

"Kit, love, please," I begged. "Can't this wait until tonight? I have surgery this morning, and I need sleep. You know how my father gets."

"Yes, Eli, I know how your father gets," she agreed. She switched off the teapot and turned toward me. "But you also know how your girlfriend gets. So think about that before you go back to sleep to dream about a girl who isn't me."

Kit left me alone once again. As she walked away, I watched her legs, thinking how much I never wanted to stop looking at them.

I turned the teapot back on.

* * *

Sweat poured down my forehead as I stormed out of the operating room. I ripped off my scrub cap. Words could not describe how worn out I was. My mind was in too many places for the first time in a long time. Not only did I have to think about how to cut into a patient's body, but I also had my father watching me from the gallery, asking questions every move I made. My romantic relationship was on its last legs, and I had no idea how it'd reached that point.

Normally, when I walked into an operating room, nothing else mattered. For hours on end, all that I had to think about was the life in my hands. A lot of surgeons are nervous walking into an OR, but I'd never had that feeling. This was something I'd been wanting to do my whole life.

"What was that about?" I shouted at my father. He was waiting for me in the scrub room as I finished up. "You almost made me kill that patient!"

He scoffed and went to the sink to wash his hands. "Relax. I was just quizzing you."

"As I was operating? Do you know how dangerous that was?" I had my scrub cap balled in my fists to keep me from doing anything else with them. "You weren't quizzing me. You were interrogating me."

"I wouldn't have to if you knew what you were doing. I'm the one who taught you everything you know. Since you were a little boy, I've been teaching you to be the best in everything you do. Why would I not make sure it's perfect?"

I could feel my ears go from red to on fire. It wasn't that he wanted me to be good at saving lives. It was that he wanted to protect the family name. Nothing I did would ever be good enough for him. I gave up trying to make him approve of me. I didn't think there would ever be a way. He always claimed he was doing it to give me my best chance, but a lot of the time it seemed like he wanted to have a second one through me.

After my hands were washed, I walked around him without saying a word. I'd only had this one surgery scheduled, so I decided to leave for the day. With my hand on the door handle, I said, "Do you have any idea how much your words affect me?" I didn't turn around, but I could feel the air shift, like he was listening for once. "I tried so hard to be like you. Now, I'll be damned if I end up anything like you."

I'd never known my dad not to have a retort. I'd never heard the scrub room so quiet.

When I got back to the flat, Kit was waiting for me. There was no relief coming home to an angry girlfriend. After my day, all I really wanted to do was have a meal, shower, and be consoled, but I knew our night was just getting started.

We hadn't finished our so-called conversation that morning, so I was prepared for anything to happen. It was still early, only four. She knew something was wrong the moment I walked through the door and that it had nothing to do with her.

"Hey," she whispered as she hugged me. She was short enough for me to lay my cheek on her blond head. Her hugs always comforted me. "I called your mum about an hour ago. She said your father told her you'd left. You really tore him apart."

"Good," I mumbled. "He wouldn't stop interrogating me, making me second-guess myself in my own OR. I just couldn't stand it. I'm not some silly resident anymore. You know what I mean, love?"

Kit looked at me sympathetically. Her family had always supported every decision she made. She'd never known the feeling I had in my chest whenever my father gave me the disappointed look. That was what set her apart from Eleanor. Eleanor understood, and as much as Kit thought she could, no one would ever have the connection El and I once did.

"I don't want to fight," I told her. "I'm so tired, babe. We…we have some things to figure out, and if you want, we can have me tested."

She laughed, probably debating it in her mind. I added, "Tonight, though, can I just vent to you about my father while we have a meal together?"

Kit nodded in understanding. As much as she didn't understand parental disapproval, she did understand long days. As the Beatles would say—all you need is love.

"I've already started dinner," she said, pulling me toward our bedroom. "Go get a shower. It'll be ready when you're done."

"Have I told you lately how very much I love you?" I singsonged.

She laughed again and said, "As much as you can possibly imagine. Now, go."

As I walked into the bathroom, I could hear her humming along to something on the television. Whatever she was cooking smelled delicious. I popped my head out. "Hey, love?"

"Yeah, babe?"

"What is it you're making? I'm drooling as we speak."

The next words out of her mouth haunted me for the rest of the night and into the next morning. I could hear the smile in her voice, the lightness in her tone. It was one of the many things I admired about her. She was always so carefree. I heard that in her voice as she said, "You should know, Eli. It's your favorite. Ravioli."

Eli

Present Day

*H*er phone won't stop ringing and vibrating. I think for sure I'm taking up too much of her time, but every time it goes off, she silences it. I wonder if something is wrong. Whoever is calling so much might need her. I don't want to keep her from her real life.

"Are we really going to talk about money or about the elephant in the room?" I joke, and her face goes white. Not that she could get much paler. I frown. "El? You OK?"

She's no longer looking at me. She's staring down at her phone, finally reading and seeing all of her missed calls and texts. "Um…yeah. I'm great."

I doubt it, but I decide not to bring it up. "Did you hear what I said? The elephant?"

"Oh. Um—" she pauses. "What did you mean?"

I look at her and smile. Her eyebrows are furrowed. I love how beautiful she is when she does it. "I was going to tell you that if you wanted to see me, you could've asked…not written a book about me."

El snorts again, and this time she's laughing at me. "Who said the book was about *you*?"

I smile, happy to have distracted her from her phone. "Well, the story is based on a little girl and boy, right, love?"

"Yes…"

"The little girl meets this kid in some far-off land and then never again. They can only see each other through their magic mirrors. Fits the profile, doesn't it?"

"It's a children's book." She's making a defensive face, and I wonder if she really believes that. I was mostly joking. Mostly. She adds, "It's what sells copies."

"Oh, psh, it's totally about me, and you know it."

"Whatever you say, Eli," mutters Eleanor. "If that's what you think, then that's what it's about. A lot of people have theories. They're called fan fiction."

I laugh out loud again, and El almost falls off the park bench. "Unfortunately for the fan fiction pages, I'm not on them. They couldn't handle the truth." I bump her with my shoulder. "Besides, it's more fun being the only one who really knows."

She rolls her eyes and nudges me back. I see a soft smile forming, and I relax muscles I didn't realize were tense. It's hard to gauge her emotions—she has a poker face. Even as a kid, she showed no emotion. It was like she was a statue; sometimes she looked so still, staring into the distance and spacing out completely. But right now, she's smiling. She seems at ease for the first time today.

She suddenly turns serious again. Her eyebrows furrow once more. "Listen, I have to tell you something."

I begin to think there's something I'm missing. I thought I knew it all; considering how popular her book has gotten, there's a lot of information out there about her, even things she might not have wanted. Everyone knows about the drunk and abusive parents. She came from nothing and made something of herself, some would say. She's an inspiration to a lot of people. I don't think she realizes that.

"What's going on, love?" I ask, feeling my throat getting tighter.

"Well," she starts, "there are a lot of things I made sure were kept out of the spotlight in order to do this book tour. I never thought I could do something like this… Once everything seemed to be going well for me, I was afraid how people might react to my past. My life— well, you know how it was. This is so new for me."

"I always knew you could do something like it. You just had to try a little harder than someone like me." I laugh and rest my back against the bench. I didn't realize how tired I was until now; knowing that Eleanor was coming to this country made me anxious. I was excited, I was terrified. The moment I saw her changed everything; I couldn't think or breathe or say anything. I'm surprised I've kept my cool this whole time.

"Yeah, yeah." She waves off my compliment. "People know about my parents. It was hard to avoid all that, considering they died right before the book got published." She pauses and takes a deep breath. "But someone else died with them. Someone no one knows about. My husband."

My heart instantaneously combusts. There's barely anything left to find. It's gone. I can't tell if I'm hurting because she lost someone she was willing to share her life with or because she was willing to share her life with someone who wasn't me. If I wasn't wearing sunglasses, she would probably be able to see every emotion I'm feeling, but since she can't, she's staring at me with her vulnerable face. She just told me something almost no one else knows, besides maybe her publishers.

I put on a brave face and clear my throat. "Wow. That's incredible. Not that he's passed away, but that you found someone that special to you. I didn't think you would. You closed yourself off to the lot of us men in your life."

She laughs lightly and says, "Yes, well, James really brought me out of the hole I was living in. He was different from any man I've ever met. I told myself I would never find someone near to my expectations, but he was pretty close."

I nod, my heart still throbbing. "I am incredibly sorry for your loss. I can't imagine how hard it's been." I pause. "How long were you two together?"

This time, Eleanor grins. Her face starts to turn pink, and I don't think I've ever seen her so happy and baffled at once. "That's the other thing I needed to tell you…"

Not only am I bewildered, I'm intrigued. I let her continue.

"James and I were together for a year when we decided to get married. It was nothing fancy. His parents and siblings were there, and mine, well, they weren't 'cured' yet." She rolls her eyes at the phrase "cured." She's never been one to believe that alcoholism is a disease; she believes that you have the option to pick up that first drink, or second, or third. I think that deep down inside somewhere, she's bitter. I've never been there, so I wouldn't know.

"We found a chapel, got hitched. That was that. We were already living together, so there wasn't much to it. We just really wanted to get married."

Breathe, breathe, breathe.

"After another year..." She pauses and glances at me, examining me. Like she's making sure that I'm OK. She knows she's already broken my heart once; I think she's trying to make sure she doesn't do it again. I was never the same after the last time I talked—dreamed—with Eleanor. We didn't know the last time would be the last time, so it was a hard ending for us. For me.

"Go on, love. I'm interested. You should've written about this instead." I'm trying to joke, but it comes out in a monotone. I have to stay emotionless.

"OK, well, I—"

"Momma!"

There's a little boy in the distance, trotting along with a woman trying to hold all her bags and suitcases without dropping anything or losing sight of him. Again he shouts, "Momma, momma!" He's looking straight at Eleanor.

Eleanor

Present Day

If Eli has any expression at all, I wouldn't know. I stand up slowly to greet my son, worried that any sudden movements might freak Eli out. As soon as he's close enough, Austin jumps into my arms, trusting me not to drop him. He never doubts me. Not for a second.

"Momma, Auntie Lana is having trouble."

I laugh out loud and look over at Eli again. He's taken off his sunglasses. He rubs his eyes jokingly. Austin is looking at him warily. I taught him never to trust anyone but me. It's a basic protective instinct I never grew out of. I want him to feel the same way.

"Eli, this is Austin. Austin James Erickson. My son. The love of my life." My arms are shaking holding this forty-pound child, and I need a break. I always need a break from holding him. He's growing by the minute, it seems. Austin huffs as I set him down. He takes my hand. "Mom," he urges.

Eli sits in silence, still in shock, I'm sure. With his glasses off, I can see the faint freckles across his nose and cheeks. Just like my James. Eli has a scar on his forehead from falling off his bike when he was nine. I remember the first time I saw it, still pink from healing. He said to me, "Now we both have some scars on us." For a minute, it made me feel like the world wasn't so bad after all. As long as I had Eli.

"Hey, little lad," Eli finally coughs up. "How's it going?"

"You sound funny," Austin says, crinkling his nose. His pale blue eyes look up at me. "Momma, why does he sound like that?"

31

"He has a name, Austin," I scold. "It's Eli. And he sounds like that because he's British. We talked about that before we got here, remember?"

"Kind of," Austin mutters. "Can we go see the dinosaurs now?"

Lana finally catches up to us; she's out of breath and plops down next to Eli on the bench. Everything she's brought with her falls onto the ground, but she doesn't seem to notice. She's staring at Eli with wide doe eyes like she's never seen a man like him before. "Damn, you're beautiful," she states. The bags under her eyes are worse than I've seen them, and her makeup is smearing. "I'm Lana, and I'm single."

Eli laughs hard and slaps his knee. "Wow, you lot. You're giving me quite a lot of surprises today."

I smile. Austin is getting anxious, trying to pull out of my grip, but I won't let him go. I know he's ready to explore this new and exciting place. "Hey, Lana, can you take James to the dinosaur statues?"

She sighs, pulling her black hair into a bun. Sometimes, when she does that, she almost looks like her brother. My heart swells. "I guess so, but I'm going to need someone strong to help me with these bags."

Eli grins at her. "I'll take them, love. No worries."

"We can take them back to the hotel," I suggest. "Meet us there in an hour?"

"Sure," she jokingly agrees. "James has his phone on him, so if I get lost, he'll be able to call for backup."

Austin is jumping up and down now, adrenaline pouring out of him. He's about to explode. His dark hair is starting to get too long; every time he jumps, it flops with him. His aunt tried to put it in a bun a few times, but he looked like his father. It was hard to look at him that way.

I bend down to Austin's level to say goodbye. He just got here, and he's already leaving me again. The tour has been rough on us the last few weeks. I miss him so dearly.

"OK, I know you just got here and you're really excited, but please listen to your aunt. She's going to need you when she gets lost, OK?"

He smiles and says, "I'll take good care of her, Momma."

"All right. Kiss." I turn my cheek toward him, and he kisses me. "Love you forever."

"Forever, Momma!" He walks to the bench where Lana is sitting and grabs her hand. "Come on, Auntie Lana. Let's go!"

"All right, J-Rock, just take it easy on me. Jet lag's a bi—"

"Language," I interrupt as they take off across the park.

Eli is watching me. He still has his sunglasses off, and his golden-brown eyes stare at every last bit of me. It makes me self-conscious about my ugly brown jacket, jogging sneakers, and jeans. I had no idea I would be running into Eli, not today at least. The last few weeks I've been waiting to meet him in my dreams again. He'd show up, look me up and down, and say, "You finally made it, love."

He smiles at me. "So…you have a son, Eleanor."

I nod nonchalantly. "Yes. He's been calling and texting me all day from the plane."

"Well, this James fellow must've done quite a number on you. Last time I heard, you never wanted kids." Eli looks proud. "You've changed. You seem different. Not happy, exactly. But different."

I'm lost in his eyes. I always have been, always will be. They're mesmerizing. When he laughs, they crinkle around the edges, and it makes me want to smile as well. I think of James and how happy he would be to see me moving on. Not with Eli; I don't know if he and I will ever have what we once had. There was so much heartbreak. Too much history. But he'd be happy to see me trying to start over.

"I never thought about it that way, but—yeah," I say, pulling myself from my trance. "He definitely changed me."

"You're still you, though. You're still that little girl I met in Central Park all those years ago."

I can't explain the pain I feel every time he says these bittersweet things to me. I'm betraying James. Going back to the man of my dreams is a little bit too…personal. I should be moving forward, not back. But seeing Eli again feels so right. It makes the pain subside.

"Thanks," I say. "I don't have a lot of people who knew me before."

"I'm glad I'm one of those people."

My lips barely lift at the corners, but I feel full, as if everything in my life led me to this moment. I've come full circle. I've started and ended with Eli. There's no denying that he's meant to be in my life, whatever the reason. I could die now, and I would die content. "Me, too."

Eli looks me over once more. "So, do we want to take these bags back to your hotel? You can tell me more about this mad family of yours."

I laugh and nod. He must be talking about Lana and her bluntness. We each grab some bags; Eli makes sure he's carrying more, maybe to prove that he doesn't care about a wrinkled suit. We head toward the hotel, and the conversation never stops.

Eleanor

Age 17

It had been over a week since I'd last dreamed with Eli. I missed him so much it hurt in my gut, though that also could've been from the brutal beating I had endured a few days ago. My body ached everywhere, and I could barely breathe deeply. My parents didn't know it, but I hadn't been to school in over a week either.

There was never a time where it wasn't embarrassing coming to school or work with a bruised face or a split lip. Both of which I had currently. When I was a little girl, most of the time my bruises and scrapes were easily covered up with a long-sleeved shirt or jacket. Now, my parents didn't hesitate to aim at my face.

Every time they did, I stayed home from school. I'd had teachers and peers ask me what was going on. The strange thing was that I was ready to protect my parents. I didn't want a teacher to take them away from me. I thought I could handle myself.

Now that I was a teenager, there was nothing stopping me from talking back to them. It only made things worse. They didn't stop until they got their way. It wore them out; they were older now, and sometimes it was hard for them to get to me.

As early as I could, I wanted to sneak out of the house. I tiptoed past my parents, who were asleep on the couch. I paused at the door, noticing that my father's hand was bloody. He had hit me so hard the night before, he'd hurt himself as well, but it looked worse than I had last seen. *Don't do it*, I told myself. *He's not your problem.*

My first instinct was to clean up the house and make it look nice, but I didn't do that. It wasn't my problem, and I shouldn't have to put

35

up with it. But despite everything they've done to me, I couldn't help wanting to clean off my dad's hand to make sure it wasn't broken.

Eli had shown me the simple ways to check if something is broken; I had asked him once. He'd looked at me warily, probably wondering why I was asking. He probably knew deep down it was more for myself than anyone else. He knew that I was scared and alone and that no one else would help me with things like this without trying to turn my parents in. He wanted to do it himself all the time, but he knew he'd lose me. Losing me was worse than doing what was right, I guess. It made me feel like a burden on him. He couldn't stand watching me live my life like this, but he also couldn't live without me.

My father's hand wasn't broken, but it seemed severely sprained. He didn't even move when I checked, just groaned a bit and rolled over. I quickly dashed to the kitchen to find a wet towel. The kitchen was a mess as always. Dishes never got done. I wasn't home enough to do them. There were paper plates and empty beer cans and liquor bottles everywhere.

Being around my parents was dangerous; my presence annoyed them. "What? You think you're better than us because you do our dirty dishes and clean up after us?" *Smack.* "You think because you're smarter than us you don't have to clean up around here?" *Punch.* There was no winning with them. Either way I was wrong, and I'd get punished for it.

I grabbed my dad a towel and some ice and then left the house.

Walking around Central Harlem in the morning was almost refreshing. People were nicer during the day, and I felt safer. Granted, it didn't matter. At the end of the day, the most unsafe place was my own home. I decided to go to the library to get in touch with Eli. I knew he'd probably already been in touch with me. He worried.

The library I went to was far from home, which was a nice change. It made the time pass quicker on days I didn't go to school. I sported a yellow tank top that I was swimming in—clothes were usually big on me—with a jean skirt and ankle-high boots. A long time ago, I'd found the beauty of sunglasses. They hid more on my face than I ever thought possible. I knew my teachers would make me take them off; it was the main reason I didn't like to go to school when I looked like a freaking raccoon. In the city, it didn't matter. No one bothered you about how you looked.

The library I went to was very small. It made me feel safe and unnoticed. Usually, all I got was noticed, but at the library no one bothered me. The computers were old-fashioned Macs, which made me feel like a kid again when all I worried about was which color I would get. There was one computer in the corner—they spread them out so people weren't stuck close together—that I always liked to sit at. It was dark and no one bothered me there. I could wear my sunglasses or take them off. It didn't matter.

When I walked in, the typical old librarian type was sitting behind a tall desk with a patron. "Great book," he said. "I've read it twice." He saw me and winked.

Walter had never been much of a reader. Just like I wasn't. He'd had this job since he was a teenager, and when the librarian died, he'd taken over for her. I trusted Walter just as much as I trusted Eli, but Walter didn't ask questions about my personal life. The only time he ever did, I shut him down quickly.

I got to my computer, pulled out the wooden chair that no one could possibly ever be comfortable in, and logged in to my email. Of course, Eli had emailed me. Granted, he did wait until today, since his time zone was different. We didn't talk much through emails or phone calls or texting or anything of the sort. It scared the crap out of me that my parents might find out and brutally murder me in my sleep. So when he emailed me "Tonight?" there wasn't any hesitation.

I wanted to see Eli so much, but it scared me. He saw right through all the pain and heartache I felt on a daily basis. He wanted to be in my life regardless of who my parents were or what I looked like because of them. I didn't scare him or make him feel unsafe. I didn't have too much baggage. In some ways, it made me truly want to love him. In others, it made me want to reject everything I felt about him to keep him away from the life I was forced to live.

Sure.

Where?

Eli always liked to be polite and ask me where I'd like to dream. I'd tell him about a place I'd always wanted to go, and he'd dream it up for me. I hadn't been to many places growing up. My parents didn't travel much. On one hand, it was so nice to see all those things without leaving my bed. On the other hand, I was jealous. Eli got to do so much with his life. I would've killed to get out more.

Tonight I knew we'd end up somewhere quiet and alone. No matter where we started, we would end up alone, because Eli would want to talk about what happened to my face. Choosing somewhere I'd never been wouldn't matter; we would end up somewhere else. I replied with the most basic thing I could think of.

Your house.

Waiting for him to reply, I looked at some college websites. I had always wanted to go to college. Writing was something I was passionate about doing, but college was expensive. I didn't even have enough money saved for the first year's tuition. Most of my money went to my folks. Even basic essentials added up to a lot when I was paying for them on my own.

I looked into county schools, colleges far, far away, with amazing scholarships for teens like me. I should be so lucky. It would never happen. Not because I wasn't good enough, but because I was constantly hiding things from my parents. Getting letters in the mail from colleges that would take their slave away—that wouldn't fly. They'd let me die before letting me leave.

My computer pinged and I minimized the screen of the life I wished I had.

Really?

It wasn't news to me anymore that he had feelings for me. I couldn't understand why. There were so many beautiful girls on his side of the world that he could have in a hurry. He was very good-looking. There was nothing wrong with him that I knew of. I just couldn't believe that of all the girls he could have had, I was the one he'd want. I was still on the fence about him; being with anyone scared me to death.

We had already gotten "physical," if that's what you want to call it. We'd been on the cusp of becoming "real" teenagers and wanted to be experienced when we got to high school. I didn't expect to be kissed, but I didn't want to be the only girl who hadn't been. I think Eli felt the same way, so when we finally got around to talking about it, we decided to be each other's first kiss.

Eli had feelings instantly. Mine were more conflicted.

Yep.

I exited from my email knowing that Eli wouldn't reply. Just the way I liked it. He knew I didn't like to talk much over anything electronic, so I wasn't being standoffish or rude. My parents almost never found traces of my communications, but the few times they did ended in some of the worst beatings I'd had.

"Bitch."

I looked to my left to see a girl standing at the end of my computer row giving me the stink eye. She had long blond hair half-covered by a beanie, and she was wearing all black. Even her lipstick was black. She didn't look like someone I wanted to mess with.

No one knew it, but I had friends. Normal ones who I could touch with my hands and they would still be there when I woke up. I had a girlfriend, and her name was Sam. We weren't super close, but we did like to hang out together. We didn't talk about feelings or get emotional. The only thing we really did was complain about our families. She was a foster child running around in New York City. I was *practically* a foster child.

We'd been inseparable when we started high school. Over time, we'd slowly drifted apart, because she had a new boyfriend every week and it got harder to avoid her judgmental stares at my parents' loving marks all over my body. Sam never mentioned anything, but she knew what was going on. It was why we were so "close." She even knew about Eli.

"So when do I get to meet this hot beau of yours?" she asked, plopping down next to me and practically knocking me over. She smelled slightly like gin with a hint of weed. It took everything in me not to punch her in the face.

"Never," I murmured.

Sam laughed and put her arm around me. "I know you don't like when I drink," she said, "but I left school early to find ya and it was a good day for it."

"I guess," I said, shrugging her off me. "I just don't like the smell."

Which wasn't a lie. The smell of alcohol was traumatic. Every time I got a whiff of it, I could feel my stomach flutter away, taking my courage with it. Even smelling it on someone else's breath made me nauseous. "Oh, lighten up," Sam scoffed. "What do you want to do today?"

The answer was sit in the corner of this room all day waiting to see Eli. I would have to wait until my parents passed out to even think about coming home. It would've been a disaster if I came home any earlier than ten o'clock. Eli would be waiting for me by then anyway. He'd probably dream a whole world up for us.

He always dreamed beautiful dreams for us. I loved him for that, and I loved him for being so willing to share his memories with me. They were sometimes very personal; they came alive and we relived them. They weren't always the most joyful of memories either.

Eli's father was not a bad father. He supported and loved him. But when it came to what Eli wanted to do with his career, his father wouldn't bend. He wanted him to act a certain way. "Don't embarrass the family." "Our name means a lot in this community, don't ruin that." Of course, I'd never met the guy, so I didn't have any real experience with him, but he sounded like a piece of work for sure.

Sam was staring at me, waiting for me to give her a to-do for the day. Honestly, it was exhausting having even just one friend. Sam understood me when she took the time to be serious, but that didn't happen often. We always had to be doing something; she never could sit still and relax with me. Unless she was high, which only made me not want to be around her.

I turned to her with no expression at all to tell her what I wanted to do. "Sleep."

Eli

Age 17

I t had been over a week since I'd last dreamed with Eleanor. I told myself it was nothing, that we were just both busy with school and she wasn't avoiding me completely. She did that sometimes. She didn't want me to see her bruised face or cigarette burns. It took a lot of energy to remain calm, to the point where I couldn't hold in how badly I felt, which in turn made El want to hide from me.

As we started growing up, it started getting harder to meet "accidently." We weren't sure as to why, but there was a long period of time where we didn't dream together at all. I thought something was wrong, she was hurt or not alive at all. The next time we made it to each other, I asked her for some other form of communication.

Never had she stayed away for more than a week anymore. The only way we communicated was through email. Phone numbers were too concrete. Eleanor said that if she gave me her phone number, her parents would find out and she'd *really* be dead. So when so much time passed, I thought maybe something had happened to her.

I sat with my phone in my hands during my lunch period, figuring out what to say to her to not sound worried, but also to let her know I was there and cared for her. At that point, I knew I was in love with her. And she knew it too; I practically spelled it out for her every time we were together. She hadn't expressed the same feelings back.

Tonight?

Our time zones were different, so I hadn't expected to hear from her right away. She didn't have a computer. I thought she used one at school. Nonetheless, I stressed all day awaiting her reply.

If she was really in danger, she wouldn't be able to answer, which made my stomach twist with fear and guilt.

Around the time school let out, my phone chimed in my pocket. As I pulled it out, John came running up to me, yelling random nonsense at some nearby girls. They gave him the dirtiest of looks, but he didn't seem to care. He even flipped them off. He must've finally gotten laid.

"I finally got laid, mate!" he shouted, practically jumping on me.

John had been seeing a girl from another school for a few months. From the moment he laid eyes on her, he'd been telling me she'd be the girl who popped his cherry. Yes, those were his exact words. I told him if he couldn't get the saying right, he shouldn't be having sex. Obviously, my words had gone in one ear and out the other.

"Really? With who?" I asked.

John punched me. "You know who, you asshat."

I stared at him blankly.

"Katie! That's who!"

"Oh." I laughed. "Katie. Right, right." My mind was on my phone. I needed to see if Eleanor had emailed me back. I should set another tone for her.

"We could get *you* laid, mate."

"What?" I gaped. "No."

"And why not? It's bloody fantastic!"

"John, the first time will not be with some girl I just met."

"Wow, you wanker."

That was the last I heard from John, as he ran down the street shouting about how he'd finally managed to get himself laid. My phone was out of my pocket the second he was gone. My hands were shaking now. For some reason they did that every time I thought it'd be El. Sure enough, it was. A one-word answer was all it took to send my heart soaring.

Sure.

*** *** ***

My first thought was to plan where we would meet. I didn't always like to plan things. Most of the time, people don't plan out their dreams, but sometimes, on special occasions, I tried to think of nice places we could go. Places I knew Eleanor would enjoy seeing. She didn't get out much. I decided to ask her where she wanted to go.

Where?
Your house.
Really?
Yep.

Now my heart was pounding out of my chest. She'd seen my house when we were younger. Now it was different. It felt more personal. She was going to see my room. She'd see how I lied about my everyday life. It would determine how she felt about me for the rest of our lives.

When I got home, no one was there. Nanny June had gone to get groceries, so I had hours to prepare. Besides, Eleanor wouldn't be done with school for a few more hours, and then she had to work. Her life seemed so draining. Not that mine wasn't, but she definitely had it worse. I mean, I didn't even have to get a job.

Focusing on homework didn't help. It never did. Usually, I did it halfway through the night, after our dreams. I'd wake up and get some things done. It was the most efficient way for me to get things done. After seeing El, I was more content with the rest of my day.

Around 12:30 a.m., I decided it was a good time to sleep. Even if El wasn't home yet, I could get a head start setting things up. It didn't take long until I was in the foyer of my gigantic house. Everything looked the same. My house never changed in the real world either. Change was frowned upon in this house. I could hear my radio upstairs; it almost sounded like a child's music.

I made my way up the stairs, and sure enough, it was music that Nanny June used to play for me when I was younger. I opened my bedroom door to find Eleanor standing with her back to me, staring at my walls. They looked exactly how they had when I was seven. There were dinosaurs everywhere.

"El," I breathed. She turned the music down. I said, "I didn't think you'd remember this."

"It's the last time I remember coming into your room." Her back was still to me. She was wearing a jean skirt and a tank top that showed a few fading bruises on her back. I wanted to kiss every imperfection on her body to show her she was still beautiful and I still loved her.

"This is weird," I said, grabbing her hand. "Being in my childhood room with you now."

Eleanor finally turned to face me. Both her eyes were slightly black, and her top lip was split. She smiled at me softly before wincing.

"I—I—"

"I know," El said, reading my thoughts. "It's why I've been avoiding you."

"What was it this time? You kiss their asses wrong?"

She laughed and winced again. "I actually talked back this time."

As much as it pained me to see her like this, I was almost proud of her. She had never talked back. It wasn't something she thought she'd ever be capable of doing. They scared her—understandable, considering they'd been that way her whole life. But considering that she'd actually done something about it this time, I couldn't help but feel more attracted to her. "Wow," I said. "Cool?"

El shrugged and sat on the edge of my bed, which still had dinosaur sheets. "Still hurt, though."

I sat down next to her, looking at her face again. One of her eyes was really red. A blood vessel looked like it had popped. My bet was that the blow had been right between the eyes. Both eyes were still puffy and purple. Her nose looked slightly crooked. Her top lip was slowly healing, but it almost looked like if she smiled too hard, it would split open again.

I had the sudden urge to kiss her as I stared at her lips.

We'd kissed before. In fact, she'd been my first kiss. I'd been four-teen. We'd planned it out. We were both sick of waiting to kiss some-one and scared to do it wrong. So we just decided to kiss each other. After that, she was the only girl I ever wanted to kiss.

"El," I whispered. "Can I kiss you?"

Instead of answering, she put her hands on my face and pulled me gently closer to hers until I could feel her breath fanning my lips. Un-til her lips were brushing mine but we weren't yet kissing. I wanted to stay in that moment. It seemed too perfect to go any further or back. My first thought was to tell her I loved her, but I decided to keep that to myself.

My lips met hers. She moaned, wrapping her arms around my neck. A fire started in my heart, or was it my stomach? She made something catch on fire. I felt it everywhere. My hands left her waist and headed to her thighs. Her skin was so soft. I never wanted to stop touching her.

Kissing her didn't seem to hurt her face the way I thought it would, so I didn't stop. My hands were everywhere. I couldn't get enough. My thoughts went to what John had told me earlier. The first girl to fill my head had been Eleanor. Since I'd hit puberty, she was the first girl I looked at in a different way. She's been around from the time I thought girls were gross until the time I found them the most fascinating crea-tures in the world.

She let me bite her bottom lip and inhaled deeply. Things were getting heated, and I felt even hotter. My body needed to breathe, and almost on command, Eleanor started to tug my shirt over my head. Her fingertips on my back sent shivers down my spine. All I wanted was for Eleanor to be loved. For her to feel worth something other than a human punching bag.

Everything suddenly felt wrong. This wasn't the right moment. She deserved more than this. My childhood room? Really? Now? I pulled away from her, but she tried to get closer again. All I wanted to do was keep kissing her, but I knew she was just trying to numb the pain. This had nothing to do with how she felt about me. I knew how she really felt about me.

"Eli," she groaned. "Why?"

I took a minute to regain myself, feeling lightheaded. "It doesn't feel right."

She was taken aback. "OK." She straddled my lap, taking off her shirt. I fell on my back to keep her chest out of my face. She added, "What about now?"

"El, please."

Eleanor pushed off me and crossed her arms. That was how I knew this wasn't emotional. It was all physical for her—a way to drown out the way her parents made her feel when she wasn't with me. Her real life was invading our dream life, and we tried not to do that if we could help it. Sure, we talked about things from our real lives. That would be hard to avoid.

"Can't we just get this over with? Like our first kiss?"

It was my turn to cross my arms over my bare chest. "Wow. That was so romantic. Please, love, say it again."

"You're being such a girl. Why am *I* the one trying to convince *you* to have sex?"

"Because I don't want to have sex with you right now."

My heart stung. Her words hurt, honestly. I never thought they would hurt like this, but every time we fought, no matter what it was, her words always hurt me. It made me want to be even nicer to her, just so she knew I'd still be there for her no matter what. Sometimes she needed someone *else* to be a human punching bag.

Eleanor sat down next to me, her hand on my thigh. "I don't want to fight," she purred. "Can we just make out for a little longer?"

I chuckled and grabbed her hand. Just like that: I was no longer angry. There was something she did to me. Nothing else mattered. "As long as you keep your hands off my thighs."

She kept her word, and her hands stayed on my face. We didn't talk at all for the rest of our dream. When I woke up, I realized how easy it would be to lose myself with her every time we were together. She could've convinced me to take the one innocent thing she had left. I would've done it, too.

Whatever shred of dignity and respect Nanny June had drilled into my teenage mind stuck when I was kissing El, because in the moments that she wanted to lose herself in me, I saw the girl she really was—the girl who was scared to wake up and trying anything to avoid her biggest nightmares.

Eleanor

Present Day

A lot of people think Austin helped me cope with James's death—that somehow James lives on in him. Only someone who has experienced such a loss would understand that it doesn't work that way. James is just…gone. And he isn't coming back.

After meeting James, I started to believe. In anything, really. My life was in such disarray that everything with him was just better. I started to believe that happiness was possible for someone like me. Someone who came from nothing, who had nothing and no one. James made me believe in a higher power. In a God of some sort.

Now I'm so angry with God. We never had the best relationship, and I never tried super hard to be committed, but I started to believe He'd put me through all of the trials in life just to get to where I was when I met James. I refuse to believe in a God who would put him in my life just to take him away from me. Austin is the best thing to ever happen to me, but when I think about how happy the three of us could've been together, I get furious all over again. Being told that God put James in my life to give me Austin—that doesn't help me cope.

"So how old is the lad? He can't be much older than four," Eli pries.

For almost the whole walk to the hotel, we talked about Lana and how close she and James had been. They were "thick as thieves," as Eli would say. She hasn't taken his death well. I'm surprised I found a way to let her watch my son while I'm touring; most of the time, she's stone-cold drunk. Sobriety isn't a life she can live anymore. We leaned on each other through the grieving process, and now that we're both finally moving on, I'm able to smile again. Lana pretends to be fine by hiding behind the liquor. "Misery loves company," I told Eli. As much as I love Lana, giving her space makes us both feel better about ourselves.

"He's five. I didn't get pregnant long after James and I got married," I say, still hesitant to talk about him.

Eli puts on a brave face, but I know deep down this is killing him.

"When James died, Austin was only about six months old," I added.

"I'm sorry, love. It's such a shame," Eli consoles me. He always could, but now they're like a knife to the heart. As much as I want to reach over and grab his hand, I have no idea how. He says, "Do you mind me asking what happened? You said he passed *with* your parents?"

Whenever someone mentions my parents, it's in a different tone, like it was their fault. Eli doesn't have that tone, though he has more right than anyone else in the world. He saw firsthand how horrible my parents used to be, but he actually sounds sincere every time he says he's sorry.

"Um, yeah," I say. This conversation is always uncomfortable, since James is such a big part of it. Most of the time, I lie to people about who was there that day. "My parents had just gotten their one-year chips. It was pretty exciting. Austin was almost six months old, so we wanted to celebrate with pizza and some cake. They hadn't done a lot of celebrations over the years, so this was all so exciting for us. I had to stay home and feed Austin and put him down for a short nap—James joined them. They were struggling financially, and he knew they wouldn't accept his money up front, so he wanted to surprise them when they went to pay.

"I didn't want him to leave. Austin had finally started to have a normal sleep schedule. We hadn't had any time alone since before he was born—you know." I hope there's no detail needed. Eli smirks and nods for me to continue. We're nearing the hotel, and I wonder if he'll want to come inside with me. I gulp. "Anyway, they never made it home. Their car was totaled. The doctors, paramedics, all said they died instantly. I was glad about that."

We stop in front of the hotel. Eli is staring at me with a pained look in his eyes. We've always been able to understand each other. We both had indescribable parents who did nothing but disappoint us. In the end, my parents changed their ways for me. I know Eli is wishing his father would do the same.

He licks his lips, and my heart skips a beat as he says, "Let's get these bags up to your room, love."

In the elevator, my mind starts to race. My room is a disaster. If it were just me, Lana, and Austin, it would be OK, but today is different.

On a book tour, you don't get a lot of time to explore, so traveling doesn't do me much good. I get two free days when I land. Mixing that with a five-year-old was a little difficult. That's why I brought Lana— that and to keep her out of my late husband's liquor cabinet. Taking the time to make my bed and make sure my clothes stayed neat isn't high on my list of things to do.

I look over at Eli. He's swaying to the elevator music. He's good at making light out of an awkward situation. Especially when he's probably thinking about the same thing I am: my room. I know he's curious, because we've discussed it before. He always wanted to see how I lived, how I made my bed or cleaned. Joke's on him, though; I never spend much time at home to keep things looking nice.

As I struggle to pull the key out of my pocket, I say, "Listen, this room is a mess. I have no valid excuse, and it will not change. So."

Eli laughs and holds the door open for me. "You know, I always wanted to see your room because I knew you were messy. It wasn't because I thought you were a neat freak, love."

"Why, thank you, it's every girl's dream to hear that," I retort.

Looking around, I guess it isn't so bad. The hotel has two twin-size beds and a pull-out. It's debatable who will sleep on what; Lana stays out pretty late wherever we are, so she's usually stuck with the most uncomfortable bed. Finders keepers, as Austin says. He's got a stubborn mind. Like his mother.

"It looks like the maid came by already—your room looks fine," Eli comments, looking around. "By the way, I love that picture."

Everywhere we go, I keep a picture next to my nightstand. It's the day Austin and I came home from the hospital. I was worn out, wearing sweats and a t-shirt. James looked so handsome. He'd had time to run home, get a good night's sleep, and shower. Jeans and a button-down shirt were all he needed. By that point, he'd bought contacts, but I always loved when he wore his glasses. We were walking through the front door as Austin was waking up, and my parents yelled "Surprise!" and threw confetti and started taking pictures. Austin began to cry and James laughed like it was straight out of a movie with the kind of overbearing parents I never had. In the photo, I'm scowling. That's the picture I bring everywhere with me. It's how my life should've been.

"Thanks," I say. "It was a great day."

I throw Lana's suitcases on the couch and sit on my bed. Eli sets his bags by the other bed and sits down. We're alone. Completely and utterly alone. We aren't in a public park, we don't have a child interrupting us. He can have a conversation with me that I can't avoid. I just don't know if he will.

"You really loved him, didn't you?" he asks, his words almost bitter, with a hint of pain behind them.

"Yeah, I did. I'm not sorry for that."

Eli looks at me with an expression that's half amusement, half shock. "I didn't say you had to be. You weren't the only one who fell in love in the last fifteen years."

Now I know how he must have felt when I told him I was married. That stings. I know I was the one who wanted to move on, but hearing the words out loud feels like a knife to the heart. How could I be so naive as to think he would pine after me all these years?

"Her name was Kit," he continues. "She was beautiful. I loved her too."

I'm bobbing my head up and down like an idiot, trying to think of some type of response. Anything. But the words aren't forming. He had no trouble telling me how sorry he was for my loss. He made it clear he was glad I was happy with someone, even if it wasn't with him. *Say something, you idiot.*

All I could come up with was, "Why are you telling me this?"

Eli is taken aback by my question. "You know, El, you're being pretty selfish."

"Excuse me?" I exclaim, standing up.

"I think I was pretty clear. You. Are. Being. Selfish." He crosses his arms and stares out the window. I'm speechless, so I just stare at him and wait for him to say something. He adds, "I thought seeing you would be something we were both going to be happy about. You've gotten to talk about your life and your problems, and I'm happy to listen. But now that I want to tell you what has happened to me in the last fifteen years, nothing matters to you."

"That is not what I was saying at *all*—"

"Let's talk about the fact that the last time I spoke to you, you told me I'd see you again. I waited a long time for you. You made me feel like an absolute fool. I'm trying to look past that. I just want my best friend back. Screw everything else right now."

I'm taken aback by how emotional he is about this. We've been civil all day. For the last fifteen years I've wondered if this day would come in a dream, the day he rips me apart for not being the person he thought I was. Now the day is here… in person. He's always been a part of me I don't like looking at. What if he always sees me as that helpless little girl who has nothing?

"I'm sorry. I didn't realize…I thought you were just rubbing it in," I say honestly. "I asked why you were telling me because I didn't think I deserved to know."

Eli scoffs. "From the moment I laid eyes on Kit, I wanted to tell you about her. There wasn't a day that went by that I didn't dream that I could. You're the reason she's not with me now."

"I'm the reason? How could I be the reason? We said we'd never tell anyone—did you tell her?"

"No, I didn't tell her. She'd think I was mad." He runs his fingers through his hair. He keeps it longer now. It looks nice. "Actually, I proposed."

Trying to lighten the mood, I say, "Tell me she didn't die in a car crash too."

His shoulders relax a little bit, but he cringes as he shakes his head. "No, love. As far as I know, she's still alive. She just turned me down."

"Because of *me*?" I ask, wishing he'd only said that to upset me.

"Kind of. It was my fault too. I couldn't let you go. Kit felt as though I was holding onto something—someone. She would hear me talking in my sleep about you, saying your name over and over. I never had the balls to tell her who you were and what you meant to me."

"I never told James either," I say guiltily, trying to ignore the fact that Eli just admitted to still being in love with me. "Even if he believed me, he wouldn't understand our relationship."

"Did you talk about *me* in *your* sleep?" Eli jokes, making it a competition to see who screwed up more in their relationship.

"No." I laugh. "There were times he would do things that reminded me of you, and I almost said your name. Just out of impulse." I never thought we'd be able to talk like this again. Like two old friends. We weren't just friends, though. Everything about our relationship was more complicated than anyone would ever believe. "So tell me more about Kit."

"Not much else to tell, really. She was a nurse at my father's office for a while. That's the only way I really dated after I started med school. Father didn't approve at first. He thought she would just be a 'distraction' from my work."

After a certain age, me and Eli came to the conclusion that although our parents sucked in completely different ways, they still both sucked. I don't remember when Eli started to loathe his family. We just bonded over the fact we had absentee parents. It was easier to talk to him about things, even when I was so closed off that I could barely talk to other people.

I sit back down on the bed to listen to him talk about this Kit woman. It sounds like she was special to him. His eyes light up when he talks about her legs, the way she walked. I can't deny the jealousy that I feel in my heart, but it's nice to see him open up to me. Lana is the only other person I have normal adult conversations with, but she mostly talks about herself and I mostly listen. Eli and I are doing a little of both. Give and take.

I feel like a kid again, the way I did when Eli and I ran through the dreamworld and for a moment I didn't have to worry, plan, think of lies I'd have to tell my parents. I could just lie down in the grass and listen to Eli tell me stories of his life and how happy he was. Right now, we're just a boy and a girl again. I laugh at his jokes, and he reassures me. It's just how everything is supposed to be.

Eli

Present Day

She's breathing softly, her legs hanging off the bed. Eleanor mesmerizes me. She has a slight smile on her face the whole time I'm talking about Kit. She slips off her shoes and curls into a ball the way she used to when we lay in a random field. We would look at the sky and imagine the clouds changing into whatever we wanted them to be. And that was exactly what they would become.

Watching her sleep, I realize how unbelievably tired I am. All I've done the last few days is toss and turn until I have to work. Luckily for me, I haven't had any surgeries, so I haven't had any distractions. My assistant did notice, though. She asked several times yesterday if I was OK.

My eyes slowly start to droop as I lie down on the other twin mattress, giving her the space she needs. Eleanor's back is turned, and I watch her breathe in and out so peacefully. I drift off, wondering what she's dreaming about.

Eleanor

Age 30

Sitting on the rim of the tub, my heart pounding, I waited for the test results to show up. *Please, please, please,* I begged. James would be home soon, and I needed to know.

We'd only been married for a few months. Something like this would ruin everything we'd worked so hard for. My knee bounced uncontrollably as I heard the apartment door unlock. My heart sank into my stomach, and I felt like I was going to throw up.

"Hey, babe?" James shouted. "I got Chinese for us. You said you've been craving it, so…"

Ironic. I was holding the stick in my hand when he walked into the bathroom with the takeout bags still in his hands. They fell to the floor, and he came over to sit next to me. I swallowed hard and turned the stick over to reveal the two pink lines.

"Oh no," I cried. "No, no, no." I dropped the stick on the floor and put my face in my hands. This could *not* be happening. There was no way James would want to be a father. We'd discussed this; kids weren't in the cards for us. Not for at least a few years.

"Eleanor," James murmured. "It's OK."

"How is *any* of this OK? We can't be parents." I paused. "I can't be a mother."

He shook his head in disappointment. "The fact that you doubt yourself so much astounds me," he said. "You would be an amazing mom."

"How can you say that?"

All I needed was the look he gave me to chase away every doubt in my mind. He looked at me with such confidence that it didn't matter anymore if I thought I would be a horrible mother. He made me realize that no matter what happened to us, we would make it. Sometimes all it takes is a look.

"I know you'll be a great mom because you had such a terrible one growing up," James said. "She's getting better, I know, but you didn't let how she treated you make you just like her. You learned from that. You grew past it."

Then I was crying so hard I couldn't see clearly, and James was trying to wipe away the tears flowing from my eyes, which did nothing, because the tears kept coming. Hormones, maybe. I could do this. As long as I had James, I was unstoppable. As long as he was by my side, I could do it.

"You want to have this baby?" I asked, still trying to find reassurance that he was absolutely positive.

"This isn't up to me. I mean, we said we didn't want kids *yet*, but I've always wanted them," he said. "What do you want?"

That question echoed in my head for days afterward. What *did* I want? Why was I so terrified at the idea of being a mother? James wasn't wrong; I was afraid of ending up like my mom. I was scared that my child would look at me like someone who didn't care or love them. I was scared my child would be born with the same "issues" I was born with.

What if my child told me one day that they dreamed about the same person over and over again? Would I be able to look past my denial and fear to believe them? Could I *tell* them I believed them? Or would I make them feel like the same crazy person I'd felt like my whole life? It was my biggest concern. I didn't want my child to have the same curse I'd been given.

"What are you thinking about?" James asked late one night, after a long day of overthinking and throwing up in the work bathroom while my colleagues whispered outside the door.

"The baby," I said, holding my stomach. The baby probably wasn't bigger than a pea, but just knowing it was in there…it changes how you feel. "I don't know what to feel."

"Is it me? Do you not want to have a baby with me?" he asked, sitting up in bed and running his fingers through his hair.

"No," I exclaimed with an ache in my chest. "That's not the problem. I just don't know if I'm ready for this. I wasn't even sure I was ready to get married."

His bare shoulders tensed. He knew how hard it was for me to make the decision to get married. Ultimately, I wanted it. I wanted to spend the rest of my life with him. But that didn't mean I wasn't terrified of the idea of being with one person for the rest of my life. It was a big step for me. Huge.

"But you did marry me. We're happy," he muttered. "Aren't we?"

"Yes, but don't you think this could ruin that? What we have together? What if we start to look at each other differently?" I grabbed his shoulder to comfort him.

"So what if we do?" He sighed. "Eleanor, I love you. I want you to have the world. It would be an honor to have this baby with you. It would be a dream come true."

A dream come true. Right. My dreams coming true would be a disaster. Real life would be a disaster. But James's dreams didn't come true. I could make them. I could give him that. I wanted to give him that. I *would* give him that.

I sat up next to him and wrapped my arms around his bare chest. He had freckles that ran across his shoulders that were adorable; he'd had them since he was a kid. I took his hand and put it on my stomach. James looked at me with tearful eyes. No words were needed; he knew exactly what it meant. We were starting another journey together.

Eventually, he went back to sleep. Tomorrow we would go to the doctor and start making decisions, but tonight, my body didn't want to sleep from the anxiousness I felt. My mind raced to so many places, and one in particular. The one place I had been refusing to visit. I couldn't avoid it any longer.

When the little stick had turned pink, James wasn't the person I needed sitting next to me. That was the thought that had kept me up every night since. It was the thought I had every time I ran to the bathroom to be sick. I needed my best friend, but he was halfway across the world, and possibly didn't exist.

Eli

Age 31

Getting dressed up for things now was just as normal to me as using the restroom in the morning. It was part of my routine. Tonight, though—tonight was different. Tonight was the night I'd be risking everything that I ever had for one purpose: a girl.

"Do you think you'll actually go through with it, mate?" John, Nanny's son, asked.

"What'd you mean, 'Do I think I'll go through with it'?" I snorted, fixing my tie. "Of course I will. I love her."

"I know you say you will. But what if you choke or get nervous? Some men don't have the balls to do it when the time comes."

"John, please shut up. She doesn't make me nervous."

But I was. John had made me doubt myself and my plan for the night. Proposing to Kit was a big step; she's told me how much she wanted a family. I wanted to be that family for her. I wanted to give her that family.

"Well, mate—" John sighed, "—whatever happens, I'll be there for you. You're my brother."

"You make it seem like she's going to say no," I accused. "Stop that."

"It's not that," he said. "I just don't want you to get your hopes up."

After John left, my mind ran through everything I had planned for the evening. I had to make sure everything was timed perfectly. Though I did have backup plans, I loved the first idea the most. Once I'd checked how I looked in the mirror for the umpteenth time, I headed out the door.

* * *

The bartender poured me another shot as John sat down next to me. I took it, letting the bitterness wash over me. My body felt numb from my fingertips to my toes, and I didn't care. Not one bit.

"You alright, mate?" John asked, motioning to the bartender to give us two more shots.

"I'm great, man," I slurred. "Just great."

"I doubt you want to talk about it."

"Not at all," I said. "Can we just drink?"

"Sure, mate." John looked at me with concern. "Sure."

Thinking back at how the night had gone, I didn't see where I could've gone wrong. Everything had seemed perfect. The first plan worked out until the moment Kit said no. With how well everything had been going, I'd been waiting for something to get screwed up, but I hadn't thought it would be Kit's answer.

How could she do this? For years she'd been wanting something like this. Our last big step was moving in together. That had been two years ago. She'd told me she wanted to know how important she was to me. I was trying to show her just that.

When I met Kit, she was a wild, beautiful girl with hopes and dreams. She wanted to do so much with her life; it was one of the many reasons I fell in love with her. Tonight, I was going to give her all of that. Everything she had ever wanted could've been hers in seconds. I never thought it would feel like this.

"'You're not in love with me,'" I mocked, drunker than I'd been since med school. "Not in love with her—I would've done anything for her!"

Some wretched love song was being sung by some washed-up artist. Of course I'd come on Karaoke Night, when everyone was either in love or heartbroken.

"You know what we should do, Eli?" John shouted over the noise. "We should shit on her lawn!"

I laughed out loud. "John, I think you're even more drunk than I am!"

"What, we could do it! Shit on her lawn!" he shouted again, almost chanting.

"Mate, her lawn is still my lawn." I laughed again. "No way."

John put on his thinking face, which usually ended in us doing something incredibly dim-witted. The act of the last singer was over, and the bartender announced an intermission. He put on something uplifting, and I started to feel magnificent. I bobbed my head and gestured for two more shots. I'd lost track of how many we'd had.

"I've got it!" John howled. "We'll move all her stuff out!"

It was the best plan John had *ever* had.

Stubbing my toe on Kit's dresser scuffed my shoes. I looked down at them a little too long, to the point of swaying back and forth. *Get it together,* I told myself. John was packing up her clothes, which left me in charge of, well, everything else. She'd told me she wouldn't be home that night, because she knew I'd want the space to myself.

"To yourself you shall have it!" John exclaimed. He was wearing one of Kit's bras on his head with a shirt wrapped around his neck. He was also holding a plunger. "I'm Super-Pooper!"

I snorted a laugh and tried my best not to fall over. "I must get out of this Godawful suit."

"You should burn it," John suggested. He was full of good ideas tonight. "Just saying.'"

"Perfect," I slurred. My jaw felt slack.

Not long after we started packing, John threw up. I called a cab to take him home, but didn't stop packing. We had a mission, and I was determined to finish it. Most of the things in the place were Kit's, down to the silverware. My whole flat was packed up. There would be nothing left for me to keep unless I decided to steal some things.

Everything in the flat reminded me of Kit anyway, so John had really had the right idea. He had my back even when I didn't know it. I had to sleep there tonight; there was no way of avoiding that. The bed was empty. All that was left was an expensive mattress from my parents and the box spring. Even the oak bed frame was hers. I collapsed onto the bed, looking up at the spinning ceiling.

Tomorrow, I would pay the landlord the rest of my rent for the year to move into a new flat. Maybe even a house. I couldn't stand the way this place smelled like her; I couldn't escape the memories that had been made here. The first time she'd come here, I'd cooked her dinner. I remembered how nicely dressed she'd been and how every time I made a joke, she cringed and laughed, even if it wasn't funny.

The first time she'd spent the night…It was one of the best nights' sleep I'd gotten since the last time I dreamed with El. Kit always made sure she was as close to me as she could get before she fell asleep. Usually by morning her hair was all over my face, but somehow she was nowhere near me.

Her hair…the golden-blond curls that she would cut and grow and cut again. No matter how she let her hair frame her face, she looked beautiful. There were times she would ask me if she should do something "new" to it, and I thought she didn't need to do a thing, but I knew that if she did, she would still look like her, just a different version. It didn't take much for me to love any part of her. Even the bad parts.

When I tried to focus on those, I couldn't think of any. I could only see the things I'd miss the most. Trying to find things I hated about Kit took energy out of me. My mind was spinning, literally, so I decided to get some painkillers and then some kind of sleep. Kit would come by in the morning, and I didn't want to be hungover, or be there at all.

The living room was filled to the brim with any boxes we could find of Kit's things. She was going to be so pissed. I snorted as I stumbled to the kitchen. The Advil was in the cabinet, and I grabbed a water bottle out of the fridge. I chugged it, knowing full well that tomorrow I'd thank myself.

The bed was a lot more comfortable the second time I sat down on it; the room spun a little less. My mind stopped racing. I took off my shirt, my shoes, my pants. Down to my underwear, I flopped down on the mattress. I felt hot and my face was feverish. It didn't take long for my heart rate to slow to the point where I should've been concerned. Once my eyes were closed, I didn't wake up to Kit coming home. When I woke up, all the boxes were gone.

Eleanor

Age 17

Waking up, I found myself in a park. It was gloomy and dull outside. My mind raced, wondering if this was a dream. Quickly, I thought of a strawberry milkshake. One appeared on the ground beside me. It was the best milkshake I'd ever drank in my entire life. Yup, I was dreaming.

It takes a lot out of us sometimes, dreaming up things. The bigger they were, the more it felt like the life was being sucked out of us. Dreaming up something like a milkshake wasn't too difficult. If I were to dream up another complete place entirely took more energy and strength. Sometimes it was harder for me to dream up things with how drained I was in the real world too. Eli was able to do it all the time.

I walked around, searching for him. The park looked run-down; the playground was graffitied and worn. It didn't look like it had been used in a while. I could hear the swings squeaking as I walked. I followed the sound. There Eli sat, swinging.

"Hey," I said, still drinking my milkshake.

"Nice choice," Eli said, slowing down. He patted the swing. I joined him. "Wanted to find out if this was a dream?"

I nodded. I did it a lot. Sometimes I wanted to know if I had been thrown out on the streets. At that point, I wouldn't have been surprised if my parents drugged me and left me to rot in a dumpster, or even in a park where anyone could find me. I'd told Eli about that because if it was real life and he was with me, I would literally kill him. Not because I didn't want him there. The opposite. He was lucky he knew as much about my life as he did. I was worried what could happen to him if he ever decided to get on a plane and come to America. My parents would've torn him apart and me as well.

Eli didn't understand it; I didn't think he ever would. I was only trying to protect myself, but he was trying to protect me too. I didn't want to be protected by someone else. It was my life, and I needed to handle things on my own. I didn't need someone to try to hold my hand and make decisions for me, which was something he *loved* to do.

We hadn't talked much lately. The last time we had, he'd turned me down. I'd wanted to sleep with him. I mean, it wasn't real, was it? So if the opportunity arose to find out what it was like to get laid, you'd want to try it, right? Wrong. Eli did *not* want to try it.

Another thing that frustrated me about him was that he tried so hard to make everything so romantic. I didn't know how to be romantic. My life was not built for that. Neither was his, but I knew for a fact he had more love in his life than I did. All I saw was destruction.

"Do ya want to go somewhere else, love?" Eli asked, interrupting my dreamlike thoughts. "We could find somewhere quieter."

I shrugged, hoping he'd whisk us to a faraway place where I'd never been. Another place I'd never get to see.

As always, switching from place to place made my head spin. I kept my eyes closed for a few moments. I could feel I was on a bed, but the air was different, humid. When I opened them, my milkshake was gone, and I was in a sundress. My heart dropped into my stomach. I hoped Eli couldn't see my scars and bruises. I knew there were some he would.

"El?" Eli grabbed my hand. He was sitting next to me in a light-weight button-down shirt and khaki shorts. He looked so laid back, like nothing in the world could ever hurt him. His expression changed when his eyes traveled to my back. The sundress revealed scars and marks I would've rather hidden.

I stood up before he could touch them the way he liked to. "So where are we?" I asked, trying to take the attention off me.

Eli cleared his throat and said, "Greece. I've only been once. This was the hotel my parents got for us."

When I looked out the balcony window, all I could see was blue water. I'd never seen anything so perfect. As usual, there was no one else around—we never got to see other people unless they were part of a memory. If they were, they couldn't see us anyway. All the homes on the slopes below us were stacked together so skillfully. I wondered how it would feel to live there.

I could feel myself getting choked up, so I looked away from the beauty.

"El." Eli was behind me, running his hand softly down my bare back.

More than anything, it made me want to kiss him. If I could forget about all the blemishes and flaws, if I could forget that he didn't want to be with someone like me, I would've tried. But I knew he didn't want me to; I knew he couldn't do that to me or himself.

Since we'd turned sixteen—him first, then me—I'd started to look at him differently. I saw this attractive guy growing into a man right in front of me while I stayed the same. I'd hit puberty at twelve and stopped growing as he started. I didn't know if the feelings were going to stick with me, but they had.

Now he was about to turn seventeen, and all I wanted to do was get him in bed. It was something I couldn't stop thinking about, to the point where I went on a few dates to see if I felt the same way about the guys Sam kept hooking me up with. When they kissed me, it wasn't the same. My heart didn't skip, and I didn't want to ask them to take me to their house.

Eli turned me around slowly, cupping my face in his hands. His face has softened since we were on the bed before. He leaned in closer, nudging my nose with his. I couldn't breathe evenly with him so close. I kissed him. He didn't hesitate, and he kissed me back fiercely. I backed him up against a dresser, knocking over the clock.

I bit his lip. It made him moan. The anticipation was building inside me. I started unbuttoning his shirt, and he let me. He pulled my dress down so I was in my undies, and he stared at me. I felt so vulnerable. I knew he just wanted to see all of me, take it all in. All I wanted to do was cover myself up. I wanted to turn the lights off.

"I love you," he told me as he laid me down on the bed.

He told me he loved me over and over again as I got what I'd wanted for such a long time. What a relief I'd thought it would be.

* * *

As I stared up at the ceiling, Eli kissed my neck.

"You alright?" he asked, playing with my hair.

I nodded, quiet. Why was I still asleep? Why was Eli still here? Why had he let this happen in the first place? My mind ran wild as I lay there with him in silence.

"This was really nice, you know," Eli said. His fingers traveled up and down my arm, giving me goosebumps.

All of a sudden, I was so angry. How could this be nice? He only did it because he pitied me. Compared to him, I was nothing, and the fact he thought I didn't see that was insulting. Telling me he loved me meant nothing to me. I'd been told that before, and all it left me with was a cigarette burn and a few bruised ribs.

Eli could be with so many girls. Girls who didn't have parents who didn't care whether they lived or died. He could have girls who would give him what he wanted: a real relationship. Someone to tell him she loved him; someone he could count on. Someone real.

"Yeah," I started, wanting to piss him off. "Now I can stop dating other guys."

I sat up, searching the room for my dress. I didn't know how the first time was supposed to feel, but I felt no pain as I got up to retrieve my underwear. I heard Eli scoff at me without moving. He sat on the bed, his chest bare. God, he was perfect. No, I told myself. Knock that off.

"Are you *literally* shitting me right now?" he asked. "After that, you want to bring up the fact that you're dating other guys? You can't even give me the respect of waiting until the next time we see each other?"

My back was facing him as I got dressed. If I looked at him, I would, without a doubt, fall apart. The air felt different now; there was a breeze outside. I could see a storm forming in the distance—Eli was getting angry.

"I don't want to hide things from you. You're my best friend."

Eli laughed out loud. "Really? OK, so telling me this maybe an hour ago would've been a better idea."

"What's the problem?" I asked, knowing exactly what the problem was. He didn't want me to be with anyone else. He wanted me to let him save me.

"Nothing," he said, rubbing his face. He was starting to get facial hair; I could feel it every time he kissed me. I wouldn't remember what that felt like when I woke up. He sighed. "Just forget it."

"See, that right there is the problem, Eli."

"What, because I don't think arguing with you is worth it? We don't live next door to each other to apologize days later. I don't even have your damn phone number. You could be dead before I see you next."

I rolled my eyes. "You know why you don't. You know I don't have one."

"I can get you one."

Now it was my turn to laugh. "And when my parents find out, you'll never hear from me again? No thanks. I want to live to at least eighteen."

Eli rubbed his face again in frustration. He didn't get up from the bed as he said, "This is why I didn't want to argue. You always win."

I sighed and walked back over to his side of the bed. He looked tired now, like I'd exhausted him. I thought that was what I wanted, but now, seeing him like this, it seemed wrong. I could feel the lump forming in my throat. I wished I could be anything but complicated. For once in my life, I just wanted to be a normal teenage girl whose first priority was what to wear to prom.

"I'm sorry," I said, for what I realized might have been the first time ever. "I'm sorry I'm so difficult. I can't get you out of my head. I wanted to try to get you out of my head."

"By dating other guys?" Eli said, disbelieving.

I nodded, pulling his face up to meet mine. "It didn't work."

Eli smiled slightly, wrapping his arms around my waist. "Yeah? Not as posh as me, huh?"

I laughed. "Yeah, that's it."

Eli wrestled me onto the bed, where he kissed me again in a frenzy, both of us desperate to forget about the last few minutes and enjoy the ones we had left together. I let him have this one, because I knew he wouldn't get it. He would never understand the unbearable feeling of never being good enough for anyone. He would never wake up in the middle of the night in pure terror, wondering if this would be his last day on earth.

Eleanor

Present Day

Since Austin was born, not a night goes by that I'm not woken by crying, screaming, or being shaken.

And that's just from *Lana*. Austin makes things so easy for me. Generally, he's a good kid. He doesn't do anything wild like run away from me or throw too many tantrums. He helps me take care of Lana more than Lana helps me take care of him.

Currently, I'm being shaken awake by Austin.

"Momma, momma!" he says, shaking me repeatedly.

I groan. "What, baby?"

I sit up and stretch a bit, trying to put together where I am. Half of the time I don't remember where and when I fall asleep. It's another perk of being a parent. You sleep when they sleep. And if you can, you make sure that whenever they make plans, you get in a few hours of sleep too. It's exhausting.

"Why is *he* sleeping too?" Austin asks, pointing to the other bed.

There Eli is, snoring softly. He looks like that same seven-year-old boy who told me he loved me. He still has the freckles on his nose—just like James—and his nose really does twitch in his sleep. I haven't seen it before. He told me his mother used to love watching him sleep because of his nose. Sometimes I imagined it, but actually getting to see what his mom saw is something else.

Even now, while he's sleeping, his hair looks perfect. He must use a lot of gel. And while he sleeps, his five-thousand-dollar suit getting wrinkly, Austin observes him. He's seeing how safe this guy is for him and his mom. It's a nice thought, but I know Eli would never do any-thing to hurt Austin. He wouldn't even know how to start.

Without any kind of warning, Austin jumps on the bed and starts hopping up and down. "This is my bed!" he says, out of breath. "You *can't* sleep here!"

Eli doesn't even stir. He's still sound asleep. Now that I think about it, I realize I was usually the one to wake up first. I ended more of our dreams than he did. This is probably why. I start laughing. Although Eli is sleeping, his body is flailing around while Austin jumps repeated-ly. This, in turn, makes Austin laugh. He's enjoying himself quite a lot.

After Austin tires himself out, he plops down next to Eli. He's due for a nap, so I figure maybe I can go back to sleep for a little bit longer. Then I realized Lana isn't here.

"Hey, honey?" I direct toward Austin.

"Yes, love?" The deep British voice that replies to me is in no way my son. My heart skips. He adds, "You OK?"

I laugh to myself. "How long have you been awake?"

"Since the second Austin unlocked the hotel door," he says proud-ly. "I'm a very light sleeper."

"OK," I say, thinking maybe I was wrong about why he slept longer than me in our dreams. "Lana isn't here."

Eli gives a puzzled look. "That can't be good."

I shrug. "She does this sometimes. She'll drop him off to me and 'come back later.'"

"Do you want to call her?"

"No, it's fine."

I get up and head to the kitchen. It *is* fine. Lana is always fine. As much as she drinks and wants to do crazy things, she never puts my son at risk. I'm sure, even if she did drop Austin off, she made sure I was here first. She always does. She probably left just before Austin woke me up.

I first met Lana after James proposed. His family wasn't from the city, so with his work schedule and mine, we'd never had the chance to see them. She was definitely the black sheep.

Lana was a whirlwind of crazy. She walked into the room and you knew there was going to be trouble. "She's crazy and wild. But she's my crazy and my wild. I couldn't possibly adore anyone more than her," James told me once. She could be sober, and you wouldn't know the difference if you couldn't smell the alcohol on her breath. Her parents weren't disappointed in her; she was just different. Everyone was perfectly OK with that.

They were perfectly imperfect. I was jealous most of the time.

After James died, though, she spiraled down harder than I did. Most of the time I didn't have the chance to mourn James because I was too busy taking care of her. There was no room for me to be the one spiraling out of control, and I was OK with that. It kept me busy, distracted. I was a mother now; I couldn't take that risk and be that crazy girl again. I'd been that girl my whole life. That was the girl Eli knew. That was the girl he fell in love with for some reason I still don't understand. I *hate* that girl. I never want to be her again.

"OK, if that's what you want," Eli murmurs, suddenly behind me. "I was dreaming about you."

I swallow and look over to the bedroom where Austin is. He's sleeping peacefully, sprawled out like he's about to do a snow angel. I didn't want to talk about us in front of him in case it got heated. Just because Eli is being sweet to me now doesn't mean that when the subject of us comes out, he'll be able to hold in his anger.

"It was more like a memory. Do you remember when I told you we should get married?" he asks, chuckling. "I was mad."

I smile. "Maybe just a little. Looking back, though, not so much."

He looks at me, shocked. Understandable, to say the least. I turned Eli down more times than I can count. Sometimes, it wasn't by saying no. Sometimes I stopped him from saying things before he had the chance, because I knew that I wouldn't have the answer he wanted. He never gave up, though.

"Not so much, huh?" he asks, pursing his lips. "Do you think things would be different if you *had* said yes?"

"No." I'm trying not to say too much. I know that if we get into it, things will go south quickly. "I would've ruined things anyways."

I'm washing Austin's dishes while Eli leans against the counter. His body is so close to mine I can feel the heat radiating off him. I try to breathe, but all that does is give me a whiff of his cologne. He still smells the same: laundry detergent and cologne. It's my favorite smell. I pause for a second, trying to focus on my task.

This can't be happening again. He can't be getting into my head again. My priority needs to be Austin, and Eli makes that so hard. Especially standing over me like a nicely dressed, outstanding-smelling tower. It's too distracting. That's why I stopped dreaming of Eli in the first place: distraction. He made it so much harder for me to concentrate on the simple everyday activities. Then it was even harder to hide my emotions from my parents. They always made fun of me. "*What, you found yourself a boy toy? No one could ever love you.*"

I clear my throat so I don't start to cry as I finish up the dishes. Eli doesn't say a word, but I know he's watching me, waiting patiently. He won't say it, but I know he's thinking about his next move. My son is napping in the next room, door open. The decision is quite easy. I don't need to think about it. The answer is no.

"Eleanor?" Eli whispers, his breath fanning my face. *God.* "You all right?"

"Mm-hm. I—I just need a minute," I stutter, fleeing away to the bathroom. "Watch him."

Eli sighs, but I can see a slight smile at the corner of his mouth, because he knows how he affects me too. How I affect him. There's no secret there. It was why we stayed apart for so long. In order to move on, we needed to let go of each other. That's what *I* thought, anyway.

By the time I'm in the bathroom, I feel like hyperventilating. It's just Eli, I tell myself. Relax. There's no way to avoid it; it's sexual tension you could cut with a knife. But it goes deeper than that. Anger, frustration, even sadness. We've been through so much together that the emotions we feel for each other are just so complex.

Maybe I can wake Austin. Maybe that will hold off the trip down memory lane. No, no, no. Grow a pair. I splash some cold water on my face to wake myself up so I can focus.

There's a knock on the door. "El?"

You got this.

"What's up?" I call, drying my face.

"Lana's here, love," Eli says, the door muffling his voice. He sounds concerned. "It's not good."

I rush out of the bathroom to find Lana lying on the floor laughing. It's only midafternoon, and she usually doesn't come home until she sobers up, but today she's drunker than Austin has ever seen. He doesn't need to see her like this, either. He's starting to stir on the bed, his shadow moving in the dark, Lana's hysterics waking him up. She must've tripped over her own drunken feet.

"Eli," I murmur, "take Austin out."

"What? El, I—I can't. He's not my kid…"

"You're right," I say, kneeling beside Lana. "He's *my* kid. Which means he'll be fine."

Eli looks sick. He's terrified to take care of anyone but himself. He looks like he won't be able to walk out the door without injuring himself or Austin.

Snapping out of it, he walks over to the bedroom to wake Austin up before things get worse. I help get him ready to go without seeing Lana. I find the pain meds and a water bottle so when she wakes up, she'll be all set. Austin hears Eli mention the word "ice cream" and he's got his shoes on, ready to walk out the door. He barely even notices Lana lying on the floor as he darts out of the hotel room.

Eli

Present Day

Austin has a wary personality. He treats me like a threat, someone who would hurt his mum. It's only him and El, so I understand why he feels so strongly toward me. He lets me buy him ice cream, but only if it's three scoops. "Momma doesn't let me do three scoops," he tells me, mocking the way Eleanor sounds. Making the best out of a bad situation isn't hard for me to do. Generally, I know how to handle things like this. Panicking falls under El's job description. But now, *I'm* panicking, trying to impress a five-year-old.

"Lana was drunk again, right?" Austin asks, licking his chocolate ice cream cone hastily. Almost like he's scared that we'll run into his mother and she'll scold him for having too many scoops. "She's like that a lot."

Luckily, this wasn't *his* mum. Eleanor grew up with parents like Lana, just worse. Austin won't have to, but that doesn't mean he should have to witness all of this so often at his age. I know it probably kills El to even let him be around Lana when she's like that, and that's why she made me leave with him. Obviously, he's smart like her, and it didn't take him long to figure out what was going on.

"What makes you say that, lad?"

Austin looks at me funny when I call him "lad." He doesn't say anything, though, just licks his cone, thinking deeply. Sometimes I wonder what kids think about; five-year-olds retain things easily, I just don't know what. He looks so serious.

"I think she's sad about my dad," he says, sighing. "I think she misses him too much."

My heart sinks into my stomach hearing those words. He didn't say *he* missed James; just that Lana does. I had such mixed feelings about my father, but I couldn't imagine not having one at all. Sometimes I hoped for that when I was a boy, but seeing Austin without one makes me grateful that I didn't get my wish.

"Do *you* miss your father?" I ask him, trying to keep him from thinking about Lana.

"I don't know him," Austin says. His face is covered in dripping chocolate. "Momma says he was a great person."

"She told me the same thing, lad," I say, with a pang of jealousy. "Your father was a great man, I'm sure."

Thinking back to all the times I wished Eleanor would marry me, I realize I can't imagine a different path for her anymore. The one she's on is the one she was meant to have, and I have to accept that. Though it still stings, I can pull through. She was meant to have Austin. He's the one thing in her life that she knows she can take care of. He's her ultimate fresh start.

"Did you know my dad?" Austin asks.

"No, I didn't. I wish I could've met him, though."

I know he's just looking for more information on who his father was as a person. I did the same thing, and my father was actually alive when I was five. I wanted to know what kind of person he was when he was younger. I wanted to know my father was a superhero; in some ways, he was to me. Being a doctor almost gives you a god-like feeling inside. I felt it about my father and again the first time I cut into someone's body. It was a great feeling to have.

"How would you like to see where I work?" I ask, wiggling my eyebrows at Austin, and he giggles. "I save lives."

He drops his leftover ice cream in shock. "Do you wear a cape under your suit? Are you like superman?" he asks excitedly. He stops walking, jumping up and down. "Can I get one too?"

"Of course you can, mate. Only for you, though."

Again, Austin takes off down the sidewalk with too much excitement for his own good. He flails his arms around as he runs, and I can't help but notice how much he looks like his mother. She couldn't help but run with such aggression that her arms went all over the place. I laugh, telling him to slow down, and take off down the sidewalk after him.

Eleanor

Present Day

I never thought I'd see Lana like this. She's a train wreck. Grateful that Eli took Austin out, I drag her into the bedroom like a dead body and pull her onto the bed. She's mumbling nonsense that I can't understand, and she sounds like she could throw up any minute. If she does, I need to make sure her head is elevated so that she doesn't choke and die.

People getting sick doesn't bother me anymore. From the time I was five or six, my house permanently had a vomit smell to it. Now she's crying, which doesn't bother me either. My parents were the same way; they constantly switched between angry and sad. I was always stuck in the crossfire. I'd console them and get beaten for it.

"Eleanor," Lana whispers as I put a trash can from the bathroom next to her on the bed. "I don't know what I'd do without you."

I don't know what I'd do without you. That gives me some traumatizing flashbacks, which only make me angry. Now she's bringing Austin into things. She's starting to make him concerned about all her issues. He's not a stupid kid; even when I deny the questions, he knows what's going on.

"Well," I say angrily, "you better find a way to, because I'm not doing this anymore."

"Wait—what?" Lana asks in shock. She's still slouched over with her eyes half open. "What do you mean?"

I sigh. Lana and I haven't talked about James in a long time, but I know I won't be able to avoid it now. I also know this is about him for the most part. He was her glue; when he left her, there was nothing keeping her together anymore.

"I know James's death was hard for you," I say. "But you have to stop this. You're killing yourself, and now you're putting Austin at risk by coming here still drunk. You're getting worse."

Lana scoffs. "Just because I come here drunk doesn't mean I'm going to hurt Austin. Why would you think that?"

"You might not intentionally, but you could still do something damaging. He's my son; I have to look out for him."

Lana rolls her eyes at me and pouts. Normally, I wouldn't care, but she's acting like a child. We never fight because I always avoid arguments with her; I don't know how to communicate with her when she acts like this. James could, though. He knew what to say and how to say it. She listened to him when no one else could get through to her.

"James would hate to see you like this," I say, standing up. "You're throwing away your life."

It doesn't get the reaction I thought it would. She sits there with a blank expression on her face. It's the same face she had in the pews at her parents' church for James's funeral. She wouldn't say a word the whole time; she didn't even cry. She was in denial.

During James's funeral, Austin wouldn't *stop* crying. I missed the whole service trying to figure out what was wrong, only to realize he wanted his father. It made everything else seem so much more real. For weeks on end, I'd forgotten what it was like to sleep alone; it's so hard to take care of another human being by yourself.

Lana clears her throat, pulling me out of my own head. "I. Need. A. Drink."

Eli

Present Day

Austin doesn't stop smiling the whole way back to the hotel. After taking him to see where I work, I think he changed his mind about me. I'm like a superhero now. He needs someone like that in his life. I know he has his mum, but boys his age need a male role model, too. My father was still high on my list of role models at that age, as much as I didn't want to admit it now. He did great things, and I respected him for that.

"I can't believe you save people's lives!" Austin skips around. "I don't like doctors that much but you're pretty cool."

I've never felt such high praise before. Usually from my father it was just a simple "Good job" or "You've done worse." Kit always gave me encouragement, but it's been quite a few years since I've had it in my life. I've realized over the years that kids are the most honest people. They learn over time that some of the things they say aren't nice, but I've never seen anything wrong with kids telling me the truth. "Can you tell your mum that when we get back?"

Austin rolls his eyes but smiles. I add, "I think she needs to hear how cool I am."

"Momma said that real men don't brag about themselves," he says, making me laugh out loud. "She says real men are humble."

We walk in silence the rest of the way back, but I can tell Austin is content. Returning to the hotel seems less nerve-racking now that I have Austin on my side to make sure his mum doesn't destroy me with a single glance. He's like my crutch, and I like it that way. I don't feel lightheaded or like my heart is going to burst out of my chest. I feel almost…normal.

89

Austin asks to use the door key. I remember how that feels, opening up the door on your own. It was my favorite thing about hotels when my family went on vacation. I was the door key holder. Turns out, usually you get a spare one, so naturally Nanny June didn't mind giving one to me. When I found out about it, I was crushed.

"Momma, momma!" Austin shouts as he trots into the room. "Did you know that Eli is a doctor?"

Eleanor, being the beautiful woman she is, is sitting on the couch, sipping wine. She's pulled her hair into a very sloppy bun, something I assume she mastered after Austin was born. Lana is still passed out on the twin bed; through the open door, I can hear her snoring. I can't imagine how Eleanor deals with her all the time.

I've admired El since the moment I laid eyes on her. She was an inspiration to me from a young age. I'm not surprised she's able to handle the things she's been through. No matter what happens, she always knows how to put on a brave face. Even in tears, she still looks strong. Watching her sit on the couch and talk to Austin like nothing is wrong astounds me. Not because she's ignoring the problem, but because she's putting Austin's feelings first.

"You don't say," Eleanor says, putting her glass down on the coffee table. "That's pretty spectacular."

Austin sits down next to her. "He was going to let me oper— oper—"

"Operate?" she asks, raising her eyebrows in my direction.

"Yes, Momma, it was so awesome!"

Now El is staring at me with an accusing face. "It was a frog," I say. "Don't worry love."

Austin makes a face at me again for calling his mother "love." He's very protective of her. That's OK too. He probably got that from his father. I like his spirit. I sit down next to him on the couch.

Before Lana showed up, I thought I'd get the chance to kiss her again. I know she's holding back now, and I know it's because of Austin. At least, I think it is. I could be reading too much into things. I just feel magnetized to her; she doesn't have to do a thing. She draws me to her without lifting a finger.

When it comes down to wanting to kiss her…well. All she was doing was dishes. How could someone be doing something so basic and still make me want her? Granted, there's never been a time I didn't want Eleanor, but I know when I really want to kiss her and when it can wait. At that moment, she looked like someone I could kiss for the rest of my life.

Obviously, that wasn't something she wanted. At least at that moment.

Listening to Austin go on and on about the frog, I decide to check on Lana. My mother was your typical wife of a neglectful, rich man. She drank herself to sleep any time after two in the afternoon. I have experience in this field just as El does. It wasn't hard to talk to my mum about things, because she acted as childish as I did. I didn't know at the time that she was always drunk; I just thought she was *fun*.

As Eleanor and I grew up, we realized how wrong we were about our parents. As naive as she was, Eleanor caught on quickly. She realized things before I did. All she knew for a long time was that her parents were sick, and she wasn't wrong either. They just made themselves sick, which she started to figure out the older she got and the more abused she got.

Lana's head is propped up, but she's drooling. Her breath gargles like she's got something stuck in her throat. There's a bottle of wine on her nightstand, and I realize it's the same wine that's in Eleanor's glass.

What happened here? Did Eleanor give in and let her drink more? Did Lana take it without her noticing? Whatever the case, it isn't a good thing. Lana will most likely sleep the rest of the night. I check her pulse just to make sure. After that, I make sure she has pain meds and water next to her—she does. Eleanor knows exactly what to do in a situation like this, but I do wonder if she ever thinks about giving up. My mother made me want to give up on her quite often as well.

It's getting late, well past my welcome. Eleanor and Austin are watching telly on the couch, and from the way Austin is positioned, I can tell he's fallen asleep again. Considering he didn't quite get a nap in, he's probably exhausted. I sit down next to him, sighing deeply. Eleanor is staring blankly at the telly, holding the now empty wineglass in her hand.

"Well, today was a long day, huh, love?"

"Yeah." El sighs. "Lana can't be here anymore."

"Why's that?"

"She won't get better. She doesn't want to. Now that she's starting to bring James into her issues, I can't help but think she could be dangerous to be around."

"Force of habit there?" I ask, in reference to her calling Austin *James*.

"It's what Lana and I call him sometimes…Whenever anyone else is around, we call him by his first name. He just looks so much like his father."

"He's smart like both of you," I say. El looks at me with a curious face, and I admit, "He knows Lana drinks too much."

She smirks a bit. "Yeah. I know. I've just been denying it."

"You shouldn't have to," I say, ruffling the lad's hair. "He should know. She's his aunt."

"I know that too," she says, sighing. "He doesn't deserve this. This isn't the life I wanted for him."

Eleanor carefully gets up to carry Austin to bed. I do it for her. Not that she couldn't carry him, but she's already done so much with her day. We're silent as I walk him over and lay him down. He doesn't wake or stir at all. It almost worries me. Being a parent must make you feel like that every time your child falls asleep.

"Thank you," she whispers, walking back to the couch. It's almost an invitation, but I decide it's best to leave.

"I'm going to head to my flat, love," I say, backing toward the door. "I don't want to overstay my welcome, and you've got your hands full already."

She stops halfway from the couch and looks back at me. Her eyes are almost pleading. "My hands *are* full. It would be nice to have some company." My heart skips, and she adds, "Just for tonight."

Eleanor

Age 15

Walking through the Walgreens makeup aisle, I realized how suspicious Sam and I looked. There was a school dance tonight, and Sam's boyfriend of the month had told her he'd sneak in alcohol, so of course that meant we *had* to go because "oh my God it will be so fun." She'd decided we needed makeup. That *I* needed makeup if I wanted to "hook up" with someone.

The only person I'd ever kissed was Eli, and I liked it that way. No one knew but us. It was like a secret. It only happened once, but it was the best kiss I'd ever had. In fact, it was the only kiss I'd ever had. I'd never felt anything like it, which is what most of my peers had said when they started kissing at age eleven. It was still weird and fresh and new to me.

My face felt red and flushed. I tried to hide it by pretending to yawn. Sam looked at me warily. "You better not pull that 'I'm too tired' shit on me tonight."

I scoffed. "You wouldn't let me anyway."

"You're right, I wouldn't! Getting drunk at a school function is going to be fun." She picked up a concealer and held it to my neck, which evidently had finger-shaped bruises on it. "This is your skin tone." She continued to look around the section, sticking things in her purse. This was standard for Sam. The difference between us was that she had the money from her foster parents, she just didn't like to use it. So as a way of rebelling against them, she stole things. Well, most things. She'd pay if she had suspicious staff watching over her.

It never occurred to me that she could get arrested. Her foster parents would bail her out, I was sure, and I knew this wasn't her first time doing something crazy. I was her backup, so when she stuffed things into her purse, I made sure no one was watching. Today, the cashier was a teenage boy reading a magazine with his headphones in, so we weren't too concerned.

"Hey, how do you think I'd look with blue eye shadow?"

When Sam was done stealing everything in sight, we went up to the register. She had a way with guys that was unknown to me. She looked *way* older than she was—like my older sister. It was the way she talked and how she would touch their arm.

"Hey handsome," she said, twirling her hair with her finger. I didn't see how that would help. "Can you help us?"

The boy at the register turned beet-red and started to stutter. "Su-sure."

Sam grabbed a few candy bars and sodas. She put them on the counter, and the boy rang them up shakily. As he tried to put them in a bag, she grabbed his arm and said, "We won't need a bag." She paid for our food with her foster parents' card and told him she was going to put the things in her purse. "I wouldn't want anyone to think we're stealing when the alarm goes off," she said. Which, of course, it did, and of course, my heart started beating a mile a minute. Our pace quickened. We had yet to get caught.

The city smelled like sweat and rain. New York was beautiful all the time, but when it rained, it became sticky, and I felt like I had just put on wet clothes. Jeans were normal for me even in the middle of summer when the heat index was hotter than Hell. Tank tops were the best option if I didn't have any marks showing. Luckily, today I was able to do that, but the black jeans had been a horrible mistake.

"It never gets old," Sam said. "Such a rush!"

I shrugged. The most exciting thing I'd ever experienced were my dreams with Eli. The things we did together were different than anything I'd ever done before. Imagine a tornado coming and taking down a house as you watch—hearing the wind howl in your ears while it whips your hair this way and that. Think how great it would be to lie in the middle of a field of roses, stars brighter than you've ever seen in the real world. *That* was a rush.

We went back to Sam's house—yes, house—to get ready for this shindig. I'd only been over a few times, but her foster parents adored me. They always asked how I was and if I needed anything to drink or eat. They never butted into our business when we hung out there. Her parents seemed like the perfect couple, and I had always been jealous.

When we got there, her mom, Dana, hugged me. "It's so good to see you, honey!" she said. She always called me honey. She thought it was the perfect name for me because I was "so sweet." If she only knew.

"Mom, we're getting ready for the dance," Sam said, pulling me along. "Let's go."

Sam's house was just as big as Eli's, if not bigger. She lived in a foster home, but she was one of the only children left. Dana and Chad wanted to adopt her. Sam hadn't made up her mind whether she wanted them to be her real, legal parents. She liked to call it "playing hard to get."

Chad and Dana had one daughter. She was about ten; I never asked, because I never saw her around. Sam didn't like her either. To me, Sam was extremely lucky. I got it, her real parents didn't want her, and that sucked, but I had parents who didn't want me but kept me as a punching bag. They made sure I knew it, too. So I didn't fully understand her hatred for her parents; I never would.

"OK, so what do you want to wear? I know you don't have much, so I figure you can borrow something of mine."

I scoffed at her. "Yeah, because anything you wear will fit me."

Sam was curvy in all the right places. She'd filled out before I even knew what boobs were. It was probably another reason why guys liked her so much. It didn't bother me; I didn't want to date until I moved out. No one would want to be with a girl who had parents like mine. It was too much stress.

Sam, though—she *loved* boys. It was all she talked about. Which was fine. I didn't mind as long as we didn't talk about my boy. My boy? Who was I kidding?

Jason, boyfriend of the month, called Sam as she threw clothes—or the lack thereof—at me and told me to try them on. She had her own bathroom in her room, so as she flirted with her boyfriend, I made my way there.

As I took off my clothes, my body ached. The bruises on my neck were the most visible, but my back was pretty messed up. My scalp was on fire from where my dad had pulled my hair back, and the bruises on my neck were from him choking me.

The dress that Sam had thrown at me was too short and showed too much skin. I wouldn't have minded it if I hadn't had so many scars. People asked too many questions. Sam said I should use it as a talking point, even if I lied. But that wasn't how I did things. I would rather keep things to myself. I liked being covered head to toe. I liked feeling safe.

I decided not to put the dress on. I knew it would just upset me to see how beautiful it looked against the background of my ugly skin. When I came out of the bathroom, Sam was lying on the bed scrolling through Facebook. She looked over at me and frowned.

"Why aren't you wearing the dress?" she asked.

"It doesn't fit," I lied. "Boobs are too small."

Sam rolled her eyes at me and got off the bed. "Let's find something you'll like a lot more."

By the time we got to the school dance, girls were already crying, throwing up, or still dancing. Sam scoffed. "What losers," she said as she scurried off to find Jason. I made my way through my peers, trailing behind Sam. As she found her boy toy, I found the tasteless cafeteria food the school had so graciously left for us. I hadn't eaten all day, since Sam didn't let her parents feed me.

"Hungry?" someone behind me asked. I turned around with a face full of chips, and there stood Kody Lulle. Kody was *very* popular in our school. He was a grade higher than me and so damn cute. I'd never had much of an interest in him, but only because he was out of my league.

I finished swallowing my chips. "Not at all," I said. "You?"

"Well," Kody began with a smile on his face, "I was, but you probably just ate all the chips."

Was he flirting with me? And if so, why? What about me drew him in now? We had one class together, but that was only because he'd failed his last semester—definitely not a turn-on. Stupid wasn't cute to me, but the fact that a guy like him would even ask me if I was eating all the chips surprised me, flattered me.

"If you really want me to, I *will* eat all of the chips," I said, smirking.

Kody chuckled. "It was more of an excuse to talk to you. I'm friends with Jason and Sam. He said you were cool."

I sucked in a gust of air in utter humiliation. That made more sense. Stupid, stupid, stupid. To think a guy would actually *see* me. He saw Sam's friend; he probably saw a girl who got drunk and slept around just like Sam.

"Do you have any alcohol?" I asked, curious to know what his plans were for me.

Kody looked at me in shock. I stared at him blankly until he said, "Um…I do, but I was hoping we could just talk."

"I don't really want to talk, Kody."

Turning away from him, I made my way to Sam. I was starting to feel self-conscious, like everyone was staring at me for turning down someone as popular Kody Lulle.

Sam was dancing provocatively around Jason. I pulled her toward the bathroom. "Hey!" she shouted, but I didn't let go. Once we were inside, she pulled her arm away from me. "What the hell is the problem?"

"Did you tell Kody to talk to me?" I asked, hoping she would say no. Knowing she wouldn't.

Sam rolled her eyes and smiled. "Of course I did. Jason said he thought you were hot. Thought you might be interested."

"I would've been if he'd talked to me on his own. You know I don't like setups." I crossed my arms across my chest, trying to make myself smaller. "It's embarrassing."

Sam sighed. "You know, Eleanor, I'm trying to do you a favor. Just have some fun and relax. I know your life is a shit show."

I laughed, regretting ever telling her the little she knows about my life. She added, "I'm just trying to be a friend."

Shaking my head, I decided it didn't matter. It wasn't worth the stress or aggravation. I told myself that I would see Eli tonight. He made me feel better, even if he couldn't help. He was the calm after the storm; he was the whiskey in my wounds. He made me feel better no matter what condition I was in.

Sam was holding a cup that I assumed had liquor in it. I took it from her. It smelled fruity but also like my parents. I recognized it immediately. It was vodka, and I knew how it would affect me.

I took a sip, but I was hesitant. I'd never tasted alcohol before, except the few times it'd been spat on me. This time, it was different. Whatever the flavor was, it didn't taste like anything but a fruity drink.

"This is good," I told Sam.

Sam laughed, shoved me, and said, "Of course it is. Let's go."

The rest of the night was blurry. I talked to Kody for a while. The fruity drink got better the more I drank, and by the end of the first one, I wanted another, which Sam willingly provided. My face was flushed, and my legs felt numb. When I danced with Sam, I felt like I was almost in the dreamworld. Everything felt good; nothing could hurt me. I felt like I had finally realized why my parents drank.

No, I thought. *No.* I couldn't do this. I knew what it would do to me, and although I was enjoying myself, I could also feel the alcohol stirring in my stomach as I danced. I could feel my blood pulsing through my head like electrocution. The music was so loud my ears were ringing. Kody made his way over to me, but I had the sudden urge to throw up.

Without thinking, I ran outside and around to the back of the school.

As I threw up, I kept thinking, *This was why they don't stop drinking.* There was a hand rubbing my back and trying to hold my hair out of my face for me.

"It'll be OK," Kody murmured. "I'll drive you to my house, and you can sleep it off there."

Chills went down my spine as I stood up, and I couldn't tell if that was from the alcohol or from what Kody had said. I could tell from the excitement in his voice that he *wanted* to take me home. I knew I wouldn't have a choice if I didn't try to find Sam, but she wouldn't come with me if things were going well with Jason.

"I'm fine," I lied. "I'm going to go home. My parents will worry."

"Come on, Eleanor," Kody pressed, moving closer to me. "I can take care of you."

"Seriously, stop," I said, suspecting this wasn't the last time I would be sick tonight. Kody invading my space made my body hot, and my stomach flipped again. I felt like I was suffocating.

All of a sudden, I pushed Kody out of the way and leaned over. Barf everywhere. He shouted in frustration, "You just threw up on my shoes!"

I laughed, knowing it would turn him off.

"What are you laughing at?" he demanded. "Damn it, Eleanor."

Then, just like that, he walked away, leaving me to clean myself up alone. How *chivalrous.* It wasn't like I didn't want that. He'd been trying to sleep with me. I was fifteen. I didn't want to sleep with anyone. I didn't even know if I liked kissing boys yet, let alone wanted anything more.

I needed to get home, but there was no way Sam would want to leave; it was still "early." Walking home would be a nightmare, feeling the way I did, but I didn't have a choice. My mind was staggering in circles, trying to think what to do as I stumbled in the direction of my apartment. My parents would still be awake. I'd have to climb the fire escape.

Once I'd hit thirteen, I'd realized I could use the fire escape to avoid my parents. Sam had shown me how. I'd been doing it on occasion since then, but I didn't want to do it too much, or my parents would get suspicious. It had been over a month since I'd used it, so tonight should be fine.

It was getting cold, and of course Sam had tried to dress me in as little as I would let her. My skirt was too short, and my shirt was too thin. The breeze gave me goosebumps. Nights like this sucked. Being alone sucked. I preferred it, I did, but walking through the city alone at night terrified me even when I had Sam with me.

My apartment was only on the second floor, so walking up the escape with a dizzy mind and two left feet shouldn't be *too* hard. Pulling down the ladder was the hardest part; I had to jump to grab it, and yes, I fell more than once. I cursed at myself. I knew if I didn't get it on this last try, I would have to walk past dear old mom and dad.

Most days, if I came inside when they were awake, they'd give me crap as I made my way to my room. If I didn't react, I would be fine. Some days, I wasn't able to hold back an eye roll or a smart comment. That was what really got me in trouble.

The ladder came down, and I couldn't help but celebrate. "Yes!" I shouted, then realized it was late and people would be bothered. I giggled to myself, thinking I was one of *those* teenagers now. As much as I hated how the night had gone, I felt almost normal.

"Eli," I whispered, remembering I wanted to see him.

As soon as I remembered how *not* normal I was, I rushed up the ladder. I pulled it up with me and ran up the next flight of steps. My window was unlocked. I left it that way most of the time. It wasn't just so I could get in; it was so I could get out easier. If I ever needed a quick escape, those extra seconds trying to unlock the window would ruin my chances.

I ducked in quickly and as quietly as possible. At this point, my head was pounding in my ears, my eyes. I could feel a headache coming on. Taking off my uncomfortable shoes and skirt, I climbed into bed.

Using the bathroom could wait until my parents were asleep. After they were out, nothing woke them up. Even if I threw up again, they wouldn't hear.

My eyes stopped hurting, and I began to drift off, thinking about seeing Eli and telling him about my horrible night. My stomach was still doing flips as the TV droned in the living room. The last thing I heard before I fell asleep was the sound of horses galloping through a field.

Eli

Age 16

Darkness and silence surrounded me. I could hear my own heart beating. I looked down at my feet: blackness everywhere. Everything was gone, and I felt empty. My body was floating. I tried to call out for someone. "Hello? Is anyone there?"

I felt strange, like I was in the dreamworld but not fully there. Like I was still coming to and waiting for everything to fall into place. Like I was caught in a middle world I'd never been in before. It was cold. I was shivering, standing on nothing. The air was thick, and it was hard to breathe. It made me feel trapped.

"Hello?" I shouted again, with more panic in my voice. I didn't like being here at all. "Anyone there?"

"Eli?" someone shouted. *Eleanor*. It was Eleanor. "Eli, are you there?"

Turning in circles, I saw nothing but darkness. I was starting to think I was losing my mind when I saw a faint light shining in the distance. I walked toward it, hoping it would take me to Eleanor. As I got closer, I could see Eleanor's scarlet hair moving around as she looked for me as well. I start running toward her. I needed her.

As I came closer, everything started to come together. The green grass formed under my bare feet, and I could feel the sun on my skin. Eleanor was getting more prominent; I could see her bruised skin and bony shoulders. I could practically touch her.

I skidded to a stop and tumbled down on the wet grass. Eleanor laughed so hard she ended up on the ground next to me. Her feet were by my head. We stared at the cloudy blue sky. There was a slight breeze, which felt nice while the sun was shining on us.

"So," I said. "What was that about?"

"I don't know," Eleanor murmured. She was biting her fingernails. "I've never done that before."

"Me either." I sat up with my hands on my lap. "I felt so alone. It was so weird. We didn't plan to meet up, right?"

"No. I just wanted to see you." She sat up to face me. "I had a *bad* day."

I felt a familiar urge to protect her. I felt every bone and muscle in my body tense up like I needed to be ready for anything she said. Eleanor was getting more…*wild* lately. Her friend Sam was not a friend to me. She influenced El in the wrong direction. There were things they did that would get Eleanor in a world of trouble if her parents ever found out, and that scared me. It was unsafe, and if something ever happened to her, I would never forgive myself.

"What happened?" I asked, grabbing her hands. They were soft and warm and I loved them.

"I went to the school dance…Sam wanted me to."

Of course she did.

"I wasn't looking forward to it at all, but when I got there, a boy talked to me, and it was kind of nice."

My heart ached. I was so in love with Eleanor, and she knew it. We just didn't want to lose our friendship, or at least, that was what she told me. I tried to be OK with it. I wanted to be OK with it, but sometimes when she mentioned other boys that she thought were "cute," I couldn't help but feel hurt. I would never tell her any of these things. She had enough on her plate.

"He told me Sam's boyfriend told him I was cool, which pissed me off. Most guys want Sam for one thing, and I know that's the impression Kody had."

Kody. He sounded like a little wanker.

"I got angry and frustrated, so Sam offered me something to drink. I should've said no."

Oh, *great*. Sam got her to drink, too. That was just fantastic. The fact that Sam knew about El's home life and the life her parents lived and still drank around her infuriated me. I didn't think it meant El was likely to become an alcoholic, but it could happen. Anything could happen, and I could lose her completely.

"I felt so terrible. I threw up on Kody," she said with a smile. "It was pretty funny."

I laughed with her for a minute before noticing bruises on her neck. "Did your parents find out?"

El grinned mischievously. "No, I use the fire escape now. It helps me avoid them."

I chuckled. "Well, love, that's good, I guess."

"I don't think I'll ever drink again. It wasn't as great as my parents or Sam or anyone makes it seem. I felt so sick and dizzy."

My hands were still holding El's as I thought about how different our lives were becoming. We were starting to grow apart, I could feel it. Almost like someone dying—I knew it was happening, I knew that I would have to let go, but that didn't mean for one second it didn't hurt like hell.

It was kind of how the darkness felt. Without El, it felt absolutely pitch-black. I felt lost, empty. It was terrifying that I cared for someone so strongly.

"Eli?" Eleanor pulled me out of my thoughts. "You OK?"

Her mossy eyes looked into mine in concern, and I thought for just a second she actually felt something. Maybe she really did feel things for me but couldn't admit it. I told myself I was overthinking it; I was just a friend she cared for and nothing more. That was what I should've kept telling myself. Instead I leaned forward and kissed her.

Eleanor's hands squeezed mine as my lips touched hers; she started to push me off hesitantly, but she didn't let go of my hands. It didn't take long until she was kissing me back, setting my whole world on fire. Our scenery started to change: it was raining now. We were still in the field, still sitting in the wet grass. She let go of my hands and grabbed my face to pull me closer. My hands were on her waist, trying to learn every curve. Trying to remember everything before I woke up.

The storm started to pick up. Just as Eleanor pushed me away, lightning struck a nearby tree. I didn't think it was a coincidence, and by the look of it, neither did she. She stood up, pushing her hair from her frustrated face. "Why do you have to do this?" she shouted at me over the pouring rain. "Every time, Eli, you always do this!"

"What am I doing?" I yelled back. "Kissing you isn't a crime. Do you not want to kiss me?"

The rain slowed. El's face started to soften, and I could see she was thinking everything over in her head. How she led me on, kept me around as her safe place, and I let her because I loved her. It *hurt* how much I loved her. I wasn't upset about being her safe place; I was upset because she made it seem like I wasn't hers anymore.

There were horses running in the distance, and I realized this wasn't my dream. I hadn't thought this up. El had. It was different from the things we normally dreamed of; I was almost shocked that she had seen a place so beautiful.

"Where are we?" I asked, moving closer.

"I don't know," she said, shrugging. "My parents were watching some animal movie or something."

"Oh," I whispered. "It's nice here."

Eleanor had tears in her eyes as she looked up at me. Her eyes told a story no one knew, not even me. No one would ever really know what she'd gone through. She had such a nightmarish life that I wasn't surprised she didn't want to be with me—with anyone. It would kill her—maybe literally—to love someone the way I loved her.

"I like kissing you," El said, tears streaming down her face. "I think I do. My life—I just—"

"Stop. You don't need to say anything. It might just kill me anyway, love." I was trying to make light of the situation. Eleanor smiled slightly, and I wiped away her tears. I kissed her forehead. She felt warm, and for the first time I could feel her body temperature. That wasn't normal. We held hands, we kissed, and sure, in my head I was over the moon, but I never *felt* anything, not how hot or cold she was, not her tears or sweaty palms.

Suddenly, she started fading. Her hands disappeared first, then her body. Something *bad* was happening. Someone was waking her up. Her parents were about to put her life in danger, and I could see the fear written all over her face.

"Eleanor, it'll be OK."

"I'm so scared," she said, trying to grab my hands again. They slipped right through. "I don't want to leave you."

"You'll always have me," I shouted as she drifted into the unknown.

I woke up in a cold sweat, my lungs working in overdrive. I suspected wouldn't see Eleanor for days while she recuperated. I wouldn't know the extent of what was going on until we had the chance to see each other next. I wouldn't be able to sleep the rest of the week, knowing she was getting clobbered by people who were supposed to love her unconditionally.

The fan on my ceiling spun continuously, but it wasn't cooling me down. My mind ran wild thinking about what was happening to Eleanor at this very second, panic and shock coursing through my body. There was no way for me to protect her. It made me furious to think that if I were there, I could help.

Could I, though? Would I really be able to protect her if I lived in the same country, state, city? Would it even matter? I was still a lanky teenage boy without a clue how to protect the girl I loved. If anything, I would've ended up doing more harm to Eleanor than good.

That was what scared me the most.

Eli

Present Day

Eleanor is snoring softly next to me on the couch; I can hear Lana snoring loudly on the twin mattress in the other room. The droning light from the telly sitcom is starting to hurt my eyes, so I turn it off. Everything goes black except the faint moonlight through the window. Once my eyes adjust, I notice El stopped snoring but she's still asleep.

It's almost three o'clock in the morning. I can't believe we stayed up so late. Eleanor only fell asleep a half hour ago; we were talking about James.

"He was really great," she says. "My first run-in with him really sucked, honestly."

I laughed out loud. It sounded like something that would happen to her—she would definitely be the type to fall in love with someone she didn't like when she met him. "What happened?"

"I was late for work," El started, smiling at the memory. "I ran into him."

I snorted. "You *literally* ran into him?"

"Yes," she huffed. "It was horrible. *I* was horrible. I yelled at him for running into me, but he still tried flirting with me. So I kind of thought, if he's still willing to stick around when I'm being a major douche, he's got to be some kind of wonderful."

I felt like chopped liver. I'd done that before James was even thought up, and she would rather be with him than me. I realized how childish that was. Eleanor had grown into a different person, and she met James at a different time. That changed almost everything.

I had no right to complain; I'd moved on and fallen in love with someone else too. I almost got married. It seemed now that would've been a terrible mistake, but nonetheless, I was happy to have had that time with Kit. She was the first serious relationship I had other than stupid schoolgirl friends.

"How did you and Kit meet?"

"Well, for starters, she was a great girlfriend. She would've made a great wife."

Eleanor doesn't seem to notice that I avoid telling her how Kit and I met. It isn't the best story; she wouldn't be impressed with me. Did it matter? I know that she has done questionable things in her past, too. Was I willing to find out how she would react? She nods with her arms across her chest. She was curled up in a ball with a sweater on, and she looked very warm. I couldn't tell how she was feeling; she just listened intently.

"I met her at a pub after university one night," I said. Eleanor already knew Kit had worked with me, but actually talking to Kit and working with her were two different things. There was a side of her I'd never known about. "It was late, but John insisted. It wasn't a bad decision at all. I mean, she was beautiful. Of course, John tried to hit on her first, which failed instantly. I've told you about John, right?"

She nodded again, smiling. "I would've loved to meet him."

I rolled my eyes and smiled. "No, love. You wouldn't have."

Watching Eleanor sleep now makes me wonder what she thinks about Kit. Even in the years after we lost contact, I found myself worrying what she would have thought of my new relationships. It could be one of the reasons Kit never felt like she was the number-one priority in my life. She already had to compete with my job. Competing with a person from my past didn't help.

Eleanor's body twitches slightly and she wakes up. I've only ever seen her in my dreams, so believe me when I say she looks breathtaking—half-asleep and still drowsy, but she still manages to pull off the sleepy look. When I wake up in the morning, my hair always points in every direction known to the human race; I always have purple bags under my eyes. Granted, I am a doctor. We don't sleep as well as we should. If we're good.

"Hey," she whispers. "Did you fall asleep?"

I smirk and shake my head. "No love." The urge to kiss her is coming back again. "Not a wink."

Her face is flushed. All I want to do is reach out and brush my hand against it to see if it's as soft as it used to be. El is looking at me like I'm acting strange, so I snap out of my obsession with her face. I focus on her.

"You hungry?" she asks. "I can order room service." She starts to unravel herself from the blanket.

"No, no," I say, touching her arm slightly. "I'm fine, really."

She tenses, so I pull my hand away. The tension between us is making it hard to breathe, and I've been waiting for this for so long that it's eating me up inside. From the moment I found out she was going to be in town, I've been wanting to kiss her again. It's a dream I've been having over and over again—her lips on mine. My hands in her soft, wavy hair.

"Let me kiss you," I say, and immediately think it was the wrong thing. "I'm sorry, love. I shouldn't have said that. I have missed you, and this is all bringing up old feelings—"

"OK," she says quietly.

"What?"

"I said 'OK.'"

Now my heart is in my throat. I'm really going to have to do this. I can't back out now that she's agreed. But I've built up the moment in my mind, and what if I ruin it? Make it less than what it should be?

"Just promise me," she starts. Moving closer to me. I can feel the warmth coming off her, giving me chills. "Promise me you won't let it go too far—Austin."

Her lips are now inches from mine; she brushes them before her breath starts to come out ragged.

"I promise, love. I won't." I don't wait for a reply. I take her head in my hands and her lips are on mine. Finally, it feels like something we've been dreaming about. It's nothing like in our dreams, where I almost felt I was making it up. Not so much the kiss or the girl. More like the feeling. They were so different.

Kissing Eleanor now—I will remember this one and how it feels. I never forgot any dreams with El, but when I woke up, I couldn't remember how her skin felt. This is a different experience entirely. I'm loving every minute of it.

Eleanor

Present Day

With my legs straddling Eli's lap, I feel seventeen again. I feel like that wild girl I told myself I wouldn't be anymore, but somehow, I don't mind now. I feel things I haven't in ten years. I pull Eli close by the collar, feeling his hands on my hips, under my shirt, wishing I could stay here in this bubble with him.

My lips feel swollen; my hair tangles in his fingers. My lungs are screaming at me to come up for air, but I'm fighting them. It's like eating after forgetting all day. I just. Can't. Stop. I can't help myself, despite every bone in my body burning.

Paranoia sets in quickly. Every time one of us moves or awkwardly hits our limbs on something, I check Austin's door to make sure we aren't disturbing him or exposing him to a scene. He and I haven't talked about any of this yet, how it would be if I met someone new. How his life would change. I never thought there would be anyone else. No, I never thought there would be anyone new.

Eli was always on the back burner. That's probably why I lost him, but he was always second-best to me when it came to my romantic relationships. Even when we stopped contacting each other, I always thought "what if." He'll always be the first person, other than my parents, I remember having in my life. There will probably never be a time my mind doesn't wander to him now and again.

James was the man I wanted to spend the rest of my life with. He was the kind of guy you knew you could rely on and trust; he made everything so easy. There was no drama with him. Falling in love with him made sense. I had never really truly loved anyone like I loved him. There has always been a side of me that holds back with Eli, because I know if I fall completely, I'll never be able to be without him. James, he made me stronger; I knew I'd be OK without him. Just because it was ultimately my fault that things ended between me and Eli didn't mean it didn't damn near kill me to end them.

Losing James was never going to be simple, and I thought that after him and Eli, that was it. I'd been lucky twice and lost two amazing men. I thought I'd have no other chances. Somehow, though, I have another one now. This is a first chance—all over again.

There was another guy I dated in college, Matt. He was so sweet and loyal, all he wanted was me. In the end I was still too screwed up to be with anyone long enough to have a steady relationship. I always had Eli in the back of my mind, distracting me from having something with anyone else.

I finally pull away, my thoughts scaring me off. Eli is gripping me so tightly I'm pressed up against him with my forehead against his. We're both breathing heavily, and his nose brushes against mine. When he lets up on his grip, I scramble off him, pulling myself into a ball with my arms around my legs.

"So," Eli says, putting his hands over his mouth like he can't believe what just happened. "So," he says again in disbelief. His eyes are wide like a cartoon character who's just been kissed by the only hot female in the show. This isn't new for me; I saw him get like this the first time we kissed—like he'd just had an out-of-body experience. I didn't think I was that special.

"So," I whisper, my fingertips brushing over my tingling lips. "That was different."

"I was going to say the same thing." Eli looks at me with a smile. "But my brain couldn't connect with my lips."

I laugh, knowing I was right about his difficulty speaking. "It was OK," I say. "For a first kiss."

Eli laughs, reaching out his arm to grab my feet and tickle. I laugh, too, and think back to all the times we did this—how innocent it all was.

We talk about the good times, the times we didn't worry about anything else. We talk until the sun comes up. We talk as Austin yawns his way into my arms and as Lana leaves with just a "Mornin'." I ignore her so as to not ruin a single moment with Eli.

He makes breakfast. Eggs and pancakes. When Austin asks for bacon, he makes that too. He's lucky I picked up a few things at Sainsbury's yesterday, or he'd be screwed. Taking off his watch, his jacket, the fancy ring his father gave him, he flips the pancakes and fries the bacon. He reminds me of James. He makes Austin laugh.

Eli

Present Day

Austin is on the floor crying with laughter—I have batter and syrup in my hair. Eleanor is trying her best not to join him. She sits at the table eating pancakes. I thought I could flip one in the air to impress her. I used to do it all the time with Kit, but I guess I'm a little rusty. That's what I get for showing off.

"Bollocks," I mutter to myself. "I guess I shouldn't try that again."

"Do it again! Do it again!" Austin chants, climbing back into the high chair. His legs dangle.

"I don't think that would be wise, baby," Eleanor says, patting Austin's head. "Now Eli's all sticky."

I watch El as she drinks her coffee. She used to hate coffee, and it never occurred to me that something like that would ever change. Something so little and unimportant. I could only imagine kissing her right after she drank coffee—first thing in the morning, while her hair is still a mess and Austin is asleep.

Look at me, imagining a life with Eleanor again. It's been a while since I've been so enthusiastic about any type of future with anyone. I shouldn't get my hopes up. Not to say she couldn't love me, but she's never tried to. That's something I'll have to overcome before I can think about a future with her.

El leaving my life because she was unsure how she felt nearly killed me the first time. I tell myself I won't let her hurt me again. Somehow, those beautiful big eyes can still cause me pain with a single look. She's always seen right through me; she knows all there is to know about me, so when she looks at me, it's like she can see every screwup, every heartache, every love. She knows everything.

"Do you want to wash your hair in the sink or something?" El asks. "You look horrible."

"Thanks, love," I say curtly. "Appreciate that."

Austin laughs again. I'm heading toward the bathroom to get the now-dried pancake batter out of my hair when something bounces off the back of my head. I turn around to see Eleanor standing with a plate of pancakes in her hand like she's ready for war.

"Oh, it's on," I say, running back into the kitchen. The first thing I see is bacon, which won't do much. As I tell Austin that it should be boys against girls, he throws a wad of scrambled eggs at me, which I block with another plate.

This is what I love. These times. Every chance I get, I want to watch El laugh with her son as her hair falls over her face. When we were younger, she never looked the way she does now: content. Her son fills her with a joy I've never seen in her before. Nothing ever made her as happy as he does. And seeing her happy makes my soul full.

The longer we wage our breakfast war, the more I never want to leave. The reality sets in that *she*'ll have to leave soon; she's on a book tour. She has a life beyond the little world we're living in right now. The dream world has turned to *my* world. It's surreal to think she's really, well, *real*.

Now I'm second guessing myself and her. What if this *is* a dream? It wouldn't be the first time I've dreamed things up that feel so real. Kit is a walking testimony to that; she heard firsthand how often I dreamed of Eleanor, how I made myself believe she was real. She never was.

After our last dream together, all my dreams seemed real, but at the same time—they didn't. Most of the time I knew they weren't really her. She was there and she was happy, but she was a blurry image of herself; she was transparent, like I would reach her and she'd disappear into the wind. And she usually did.

This Eleanor *is* real. Standing in front of me now, armed with a bottle of syrup, she's real. She makes it possible for me to believe that again. Austin makes it possible to believe; I can't have dreamed *him* up. I couldn't think someone up like that. He was real, so she was real. All of this was real, and I was in the middle of it.

For once in my life, I was happy to be awake.

Eli

Age 22

But you *did* love her, didn't you?" my therapist asked as I stared at his watch. The hands were moving slower than I thought possible.

"Sure I did," I said, shrugging. "But she wasn't real, right?"

"Is that what you think?" he countered. "Do you really believe that?"

I sighed deeply. Since Eleanor left my dreams—my life—I'd been seeing a therapist. My parents could tell that I was getting depressed; they knew I was heartbroken. They had no idea who the girl was, or that there even was a girl, but sure enough, her disappearance had made my life a living hell.

"Aren't you supposed to be convincing me otherwise?"

Don smiled at me. Yes, I called him by his first name. He'd said it would be better if we were more like friends. We could be more comfortable with each other. "Just because it happened in your head doesn't mean it didn't happen."

Don turned everything around on me. That's what therapists do. He liked to do it often and usually it worked. Usually, I fell for it.

I wanted him to tell me Eleanor wasn't real. I wanted him to tell me there was something wrong with me. My first day here, I told him the real reason. He didn't look at me like I was crazy or on drugs. He looked at me like I was heartbroken.

"Don, it didn't happen," I said. "Eleanor was just some brain malfunction. That's all."

"And why do you think that, Eli?"

121

"It hurts too damn much to think otherwise."

Don stared at me blankly, then wrote something down on his stupid clipboard. He was always scribbling things down when he thought I wasn't looking. I was *always* looking.

"So you're telling me," he began, crossing his arms across his needlepoint sweater, "that if you *did* believe Eleanor was real, you couldn't handle the pain?"

I nodded. "She broke me. I mean, I did it to myself. This figment of my imagination broke my heart, and I can't even think how that could really happen. I can't fathom how someone who claimed to love me could hurt me like that."

"Isn't that what makes it real? That it hurts?" Don questioned. "To me, and this is a personal opinion, not a therapist's opinion, I would've rather lost a real girl than an imaginary one. For some reason you'd rather be mad than admit she existed."

"I *am* mad, Don. There's no other explanation for this."

"You were in love," Don said. "That's the *only* explanation for this."

"What d'you mean?"

"What do I mean? Love makes you mad, Eli." Don set down his clipboard and leaned forward. "Have you ever thought that maybe, just maybe, it was real *because* of your feelings? That none of this could be possible if it wasn't real—if Eleanor wasn't real?"

I'd never thought about it like that. Most days, I was too busy trying to tell myself that she wasn't real just to avoid the pain. If I had told anyone else, I would've been mad, but Don made me feel like I wasn't. He made my feelings valid. Which *was* his job.

"Have you been eating better and exercising again?" he asked.

"As much as I can now with university in the way," I said, thinking about the stress my father was putting me under. "It's hard."

Don smiled. "As long as you're trying. I can't scold you for trying."

Don talked to me more about Eleanor and how I should accept that she was a real, active part of my life. She wasn't just a dream. Never in my life had I thought myself to be normal. Sitting with Don, playing chess and just talking, made all the difference. I'd never had anyone to talk to about Eleanor. Granted, now it was too late.

She was becoming a distant memory. When we—she—decided that our "friendship" wasn't working, I tried like hell to fight for what I thought we had. But her mind was already made up. I could tell that her feelings toward me were changing.

I should've gone to therapy sooner.

No one wants to admit there's something wrong with them. It took my parents to notice how depressed I was. That was a shocking thing, too; they never noticed anything except how school was going.

"So, what are you going to do this week?" Don asked, moving his knight to attack one of my pawns.

"'Admit to myself I was actually in love with a real person and that even though she hurt me, the experiences I had with her were some of the best I've ever had,'" I mocked Don as he beat me in chess. "Damn, you're too good."

Don laughed. "I've been at this a while."

When my session was over, there wasn't a lot of time to dillydally. Don was too popular; people—rich and poor, famous and ordinary—came to him. I was surprised by the people I ran into in a therapist's office.

It was rainy in London, go figure, so I took the tube. It was quiet and packed with all kinds of people in their own worlds thinking about things completely different from me. A girl with light blond hair cut to her shoulders flirted with me from across the train car, gesturing to me to sit next to her. Feeling my face get warm, I turned away. Next to me, an old man was falling asleep standing up. He looked like he'd just finished a hard day at work somewhere that didn't pay him nearly enough to afford a car.

Thinking about the different people made me think of the only person I wished was standing next to me. *Eleanor.* I wondered if she'd be jealous at the way the blond girl stared at me. I wondered if she'd care that I gave in and sat next to the girl the rest of the way home.

As the tube population slowly thinned, me and the girl got closer. We laughed more often, touched more often. She was fun; her stories were wild. For once, I wasn't thinking about Eleanor and wondering how she was feeling. What might set her off and make her unhappy.

I missed my stop as the girl kissed me softly. The train car was empty except for us. When we got to her stop, she invited me back with her so we could continue to get to know each other. Every inch, every dip or curve of body—my skin burned at her touch.

The rest of the night I didn't want to think about anything but what was happening in the moment. *Shit*, I thought, *I need therapy*. All I was supposed to do was tell myself that Eleanor had been the first girl I loved and that no matter what, she was real, and the pain she caused meant that I'd had good experiences with her.

That was the last time I went to therapy.

Eleanor

Age 28

I was sweating through everything I was wearing. I swore under my breath. My date with James was tonight—my *first*—and I couldn't figure out what the hell to wear. Nervous sweating had become a personal issue for me as I grew up; my parents made it hard to *not* sweat. My cat, Tubbs, watched me struggle into jeans that wouldn't slide up because I couldn't stop *sweating*.

"He's going to be here any minute," I mumbled to myself and Tubbs.

James wanted to be a gentleman and "pick me up." Obviously, since we lived in New York, picking me up meant meeting me at my house. I'd told him I wanted to meet somewhere else; I didn't want anyone knowing where I lived just yet. I was a very private person; not a day went by that I wasn't terrified my parents would find me.

There was a knock at the door, and I was still in my underwear. My feline friend was meowing at the door—imagine that, a cat "barking" at the door—making me sweat even more.

"Stop, Tubbs," I whispered.

I threw on a sundress, thinking that would give me the most breeze. It would keep me from getting so uncomfortable I wouldn't be able to think about anything but the sweat. Tubbs was staring at me as if to say, "You're wearing *that?*"

I shrugged at my cat and opened the door. James was wearing a leather jacket with his hair tied back. He looked relaxed, like he wasn't trying at all. In his hand was one single flower. A sunflower.

"Just one?" I said, smiling. The sunflower looked just the way it should. Something you didn't often get in the city.

"I didn't want to seem like an overachiever on the first date."

Tubbs meowed as I shut the door. James had a place set up for us to eat. I wasn't expecting a rooftop date and three-course meal. The food was catered from somewhere I could never afford. That wasn't something men did often, but when they did, how could you not be in awe?

The food was amazing, and James was a gentleman.

"So what do you do?" he asked while we were eating the first course: salad.

"I work at an editorial company. I just do office work. Not an actual editor."

"But you want to be?"

I shrugged, not knowing the answer. "I applied anywhere I could when I first moved out of my parents'. It was the first job I was offered. Maybe I'll write a book one day."

Just acknowledging my parents' existence was nerve-racking. If he asked about them, I couldn't lie. Or didn't want to. They didn't deserve it. No, I never brought them up on my own—it hurt too much—but if someone else mentioned them, I didn't hold back.

"What about you?" I asked, avoiding the subject. "What do you do?"

James went on to tell me he was an architect for an eco-friendly company. Go figure. "They're really great. I design things for their buildings. I actually helped design the one we're on right now."

Wow. It made sense now why we'd been allowed up here; it looked like the building was vacant.

"Do you make a lot of money?" I asked bluntly. James laughed, choking on his soup, and I added, "I'm sorry. That was rude."

He waved off my apology. "It's fine. I don't mind. It's just surprising you ask."

I smiled. "So do you?"

"I do, yes." James laughed and shook his head. "Enough to live comfortably."

We finished our whole meal while getting to know each other; it seemed like everything he did was an adventure or exciting. My life was dull, and I made sure he knew that.

"It can't be that bad," James tried to convince me as we walked back to my apartment. It wasn't far, which was nice; it was getting cold. *Way to go with the dress.* "Your life seems interesting to me."

I snorted and said, "You must be desperate to think *I'm* interesting."

James said nothing. I started to panic, thinking I had pushed too far. I shouldn't have said that I wasn't so interesting. He probably thought I wanted nothing to do with him now. That I'd said that stuff to make sure he stayed away from me. The truth was the opposite; I was enjoying myself *so* much. I just wanted him to know what he was getting himself into. I wanted him to know that I wasn't the amazing and vivacious girl he seemed to think I was. I didn't want to disappoint him.

We were almost back to my apartment, and still we hadn't said a word. I could hear someone throwing up not too far from us. It had become a familiar sound. People got sick in New York all the time—drunk, sober, it didn't matter. But there was something about *this* person throwing up that stopped me in my tracks. My legs went numb, and I couldn't move. My breathing became labored; my lungs felt like they were failing. James had already noticed a change before we stopped moving, but now he was concerned.

"You OK, Eleanor? What's wrong?"

My parents. I tried to talk but the words wouldn't come out of my mouth. *They found me.* How? I'd been so careful. I made sure not to give out my address, and no one at work knew who they were.

"Do you know 'em?" James asked. All I could do was nod. I had nothing in me but paralyzing fear. He said, "Stay here."

I hid behind a nearby staircase, praying to God James could make them leave.

"Where is she?" I heard my mother shout. "She can't be far from here if you were with her."

I tried to mold myself into the staircase, hoping she'd be too drunk to recognize me. If only that were the case.

"There you are," she slurred. Of course she was drunk. What was that supposed to change? "I need to speak with you."

"I'm sorry, Eleanor. I already had to hit the guy." James was standing behind my sickly mother, tense, with an already bruised hand. He looked ready to pounce at any moment. My mom was standing over me. She was terrifying even when she was sober. Even more when she wasn't. "Speak with me" usually meant hurt me.

"What do you want, Pat? What can I do for *you*?" I choked out, straightening up to make myself a little taller.

She looked shocked as she took a step back from me. "We—your father and me—need your help. We have a problem, and we need help."

No kidding. Standing in front of her, I noticed how pathetic she looked. Pat was the skinniest she'd ever been, and she could barely stand up straight. From the look of things, I wouldn't have been surprised if she'd told me she was dying.

"You've always needed help, *Mom*. I tried to help you." I found some courage in my heart. "I'm done trying. You and Dad need to go back into whatever hole you crawled out of."

Pushing past her, I held out my hand for James to take. He gladly did, grabbing my hand with his good one. We started to walk off.

Pat followed us. "That's not good enough, ol' daughter of mine."

James tightened his grip and kept walking.

"You can't just ignore me. I'm still your mother!"

I felt a grip on my scalp. James didn't catch it in time, and my mother turned me to her with my head pulled back. Her palm came down on my cheek. I felt my lip split. It had been a long time since I'd been slapped, but it still stung just as much. Physically and emotionally.

"What the hell is wrong with you?" James shouted, pushing her away. She pulled some of my hair out as she plopped on the ground. "Stay away from her, both of you. I will not hesitate to call the cops."

Pat laughed, struggling to balance herself as she stood up with my hair still in her clenched fist. "Whatever. We were hoping our daughter would help us get into a rehab facility, but I guess she still disappoints us. Come on, Bill."

She pulled my dad away. I could barely breathe and my face throbbed. I could hear ringing in my ears as James rubbed my back softly. Tears rolled down my hot face, cooling my throbbing cheek, making me realize I was still on a *date*. My real first date was ruined because of my parents. All this time, I'd hidden away from men, and the one time I decided there was no harm, I got slapped in the face.

"Your life isn't interesting, huh?" James asked. "Come on, let's get you inside so I can look at your cheek."

"You still want to 'get me inside,' even after all that? You *must* be desperate."

James smiled and said, "Not desperate. Interested."

We got to my apartment door and I started to sweat again. I saw where this was going, and honestly, I didn't need help with my face. I'd had worse damage over the years. He wanted to come *in*. See my apartment. Learn who I was. He might even want more than that.

"OK," I mumbled, pulling out my keys. "This is probably the best time to say goodnight."

"Not ready for me to come in?" James said, leaning closer.

I hadn't kissed in a year. I'd had a fling in college, but it didn't last long enough to say it was genuine. I hadn't kissed anyone I genuinely liked since…Eli.

Now I was thinking about Eli. Great.

James put his hand on my hip, pulling me in. I was at a loss for words. I could feel his breath on my face; I knew he was waiting for me to give him the OK to kiss me. I noticed the way he smelled for the first time. His shirt smelled so strong it was intoxicating. I nudged my nose to his, and his lips touched mine.

I couldn't describe what I was feeling. There had been so many emotions running through my head on the walk home. It felt so nice to kiss someone again. I'd missed it more than I knew.

James wrapped his arms around me and moaned softly. I tangled my hands in his long hair. It was soft, nicer than my own. Warmth radiated off him, and my face heated. I felt hot everywhere, from head to toe.

I was squirming in anticipation as his hands started to roam. We were in the hallway of my apartment complex. Shit. James's hands started to make their way up my thighs and under my dress. I pulled away, or tried to. His hands didn't move an inch.

"I, um," I stuttered, "I think we shouldn't be outside."

James's forehead leaned on mine. My back was pressed against the door. If I listened hard enough, I could hear Tubbs calling for me. He laughed breathlessly. "Still don't want me to come in?"

His gray-blue eyes met mine, and I saw every reassurance that I needed to know this was more than a hookup. For some reason I was still trying to understand, James *cared* about me.

After everything that had happened tonight with my parents, I didn't want to be alone. What better way than to spend the night with the person who had been there? I was still in shock. Once it all settled in, I thought I might have a panic attack.

At that point, I didn't care what he wanted. Sex, friendship, *love*. I'd do what I could to keep him with me, even if it was just for the night. I felt safe with him the way I'd never been with a living, breathing person. He'd *punched* my dad. If my parents came back, I'd feel OK being with him.

James was still looking into my eyes when I said, "I never said that." He smiled and pulled away just enough for me to unlock my front door. He whispered sweet nothings in my ear as we grabbed ice for my face and his hand. We took it to my room so he could do everything he had in mind.

Tubbs joined us as I told him about the abuse of my childhood. He looked at me like he found it inspiring that I'd made it this far alone. At one point he said, "You had absolutely no one."

I could've told him about Eli. I didn't have to say he was in my dreams. But for some reason I wanted to keep him a secret. He was *my* secret, and I liked it that way.

"You are the most beautiful girl I've ever met," James whispered to me as we fell asleep with my furry friend between us. "I hope you know how interested I truly am. You are something else, Eleanor Scott."

We fell asleep with our clothes *on*. Imagine that.

* * *

In the morning, my nostrils flooded with the smell of smoke. *Burnt food*. The last time I'd smelled burnt food was when my mother and father got so blackout drunk that they passed out with the stove on. I was twelve and not nearly as surprised as I should've been.

Tubbs wasn't in the room with me, which worried me. My instinct was to flee, but instead, I made myself run to the kitchen. I found James desperately trying to make breakfast. He had flour in his hair, which could only mean he was making pancakes or biscuits. I hoped for both.

I watched him for a few minutes, unnoticed. He had a worried expression like he couldn't get anything right. I'd be nervous, too, having to cook for someone I'd just spent the night with. He was stirring things and cracking eggs. At one point, bacon grease splattered his shirt, and I giggled.

"Uh," I finally said. "How's it going?"

James looked up and laughed nervously. "I almost burned down your apartment a few minutes ago."

"I smelled that. Why don't you let me help?"

Tubbs came trotting over to me. He rubbed against my legs, and I realized I'd just woken up. My hair was in a messy bun that looked like an octopus was sitting on my head, and my dress was wrinkled. Not to mention the sweatpants I'd thrown on underneath.

Aware that James was not staring at my sense of style, I slowly turned back to my bedroom to change. Of course, Tubbs joined me.

"He's still here," I whispered to him. "Why is he still here?"

The expression I got from Tubbs looked like he was trying to say, "Are you kidding me?" Like I was crazy to wonder. Tubbs practically rolled his eyes as he bounced onto my bed.

A normal day of clothes for me was jeans and a T-shirt, which was what James had met me in, so there was no point trying to impress him. He'd gotten to see my fancy side last night.

Last night. My parents. I'd forgotten about them until now. I checked my face in the mirror. Bruised, with my mother's signature mark: a split lip. I rubbed my tongue against it. It stung.

There were things my parents had done that were unforgivable, but this took the cake. It had been years—*ten years*—since I'd seen them. At the age of eighteen, I'd moved out of their apartment and lived with Sam until I got my job in the editorial department. For them to find me now, when they hadn't changed—I was devastated. They were still trying to use me. They wanted me to pay for their re-hab. They had no money or jobs. The only thing they knew how to do was steal and hustle.

"I hate them, Tubbs."

He meowed at me.

"I *hate* them."

I returned to the kitchen, where James seemed to have a handle on the pancake situation. It smelled fluffy with a side of crispy. *Bacon.* He wore the floral apron I never used. I was glad it was getting put to good use.

I sat down on the stool at the kitchen bar. I didn't have a dining ta-ble; I was the only one who ate here besides Tubbs. James told me he'd fed the cat already and cleaned up whatever mess we'd made the night before with snacks.

"Thanks," I said anxiously. I'd never had anyone want to take care of me before. Except Eli, who never could.

As we ate our pancakes, James stared at my face. "Your mom can really throw a punch, huh?" He touched my face softly, and I winced.

Snorting, I said, "You don't know half of it."

He got serious, his eyebrows furrowing. "If you don't mind me asking—what was the worst thing they've done to you?"

My mind wandered back to all the times I'd been afraid I was going to die. I was younger then, but I hadn't thought my parents would know when to stop. Luckily, they always did, but more because they were getting worn out.

Did I really want to tell James something so personal? My life may seem interesting right now to him, but what if I opened up and it was too much for him? What if he couldn't handle what a train wreck I was? Taking the risk telling him such a big, detailed part of my past made me want to run away.

How could I ever move on from Eli if I treated everyone just like him? I never had a serious relationship because I couldn't stand the thought of letting someone close enough to me, telling them the scary things. This time it should be different, this time I could show someone who I really am and my past.

"I dislocated my knee once," I said. James's eyes widened like a deer caught in the headlights. I amended, "Well, my dad did."

"How did that even happen? I can't even imagine."

I shrugged. "I was hiding from him. I don't even remember what he was angry about, but I remember him looking for me. I had hiding spots all over the house. This time, I hid in a tall cabinet, and unfortunately, he didn't tire out before finding me.

"When he pulled me out, he dropped me. My knee hit the ground first. Popped right out."

"Wow," he murmured. "That's horrible."

I laughed. "That's not even the worst part. He didn't stop at that. He got a couple kicks in."

James didn't say anything after that, just started shaking his head. He cleaned up for me and told me to go relax. Whatever that meant. I didn't know how to relax after last night.

After the dishes were done, he came to sit next to me on the couch. He put his head in my lap like he was contemplating life. Almost like we had known each other for years. "Do you ever wish you had a different life?"

He wasn't looking at me when he asked. I felt pain in my chest. On one hand, I would've loved to have any other life than the one I'd had. On the other, I didn't think I would've ever met Eli. As much as I couldn't stand to think about him, I wouldn't have wanted to *not* know him.

"Do you?" I avoided the question.

"Sometimes," James admitted. "My family—whom I hope you'll get to meet—is exhausting. I love them to death, but sometimes, if I didn't have a family at all, I'd be OK with that too."

I was almost jealous. I'd always been jealous when Sam complained about her family, and I guess it was because I never had one of my own. I was old enough to understand that everyone needs a break now and then, but I'd rather be with one than without. It gets lonely.

"You want me to meet them, huh?" I asked. "Even if they exhaust you?"

"Even then," James said, smiling. "Even if you exhausted me, I'd still want to have you in my life too."

He pulled me down, and I kissed him until Tubbs got jealous and jumped between us. It was Saturday with nothing to do but get to know each other; we watched TV and kissed some more. James told me about his wildflower black-sheep sister and his reserved brother—both younger. His mother's family was rich, but his father's wasn't. She'd left her family's money to be with him, and their relationship had never faltered.

"I hope one day I can find that," James murmured as he wrapped his arms around me. "I hope I can find that with you."

No pressure.

Eleanor

Present Day

A ustin is licking his ice cream so quickly I think it'll fall off the cone. After Eli left, I decided I needed to explain things to Austin the best I could. He didn't seem to mind Eli and the closeness we shared, but I knew I'd feel better if we talked.

Eli said he had some errands to run and if I gave him my number, he'd most certainly call me. As much as I believed he would, I just told him to meet me at the park with Austin when he was done. Call me paranoid, but the last time I found love, he died.

The day James died, I told myself I wouldn't be able to open myself up to anyone again. At the end of the day, I hadn't even fully opened myself to him—I'd never told him about Eli—but it was the closest I'd come. He was my rock; he made everything feel different. He never made me feel like I was doing something wrong. He never made me feel unloved.

In some ways, I felt like I was betraying him. Being with Eli seemed wrong. I'd made my bed and slept in it, but this time—this was different. I needed Austin to tell me it was OK to move on.

"Slow down, boy," I tell Austin, ruffling his dark hair. "You act like I never give you ice cream."

"Not. Three. Scoops!" Austin exclaims between licks. He makes a suspicious face. "Eli gave me three scoops yesterday. Don't tell him I told you!"

I laugh. I knew he would do something to bribe my son, and if three scoops of ice cream were the worst of it, I could manage. "I'll make sure to keep it a secret." I pause. Now would be as good a time as any. "What do you think of him? Of Eli?"

Austin just shrugs. "He's OK."

"Just OK?"

He shrugs again.

"Well," I say, "who do you think he is to me?"

His eyebrows smoosh together like he's thinking. He looks so much like his father when he does that. Always concentrating. "I don't know," he says. "Your boyfriend?"

As bad as it sounds, I'm relieved he already thinks that. Granted, it isn't true, but I don't want him to think less of Eli either. I'm not sure where things are going, so I don't want him to think either way.

"Well, no," I say. "He's just a friend right now. I'm not sure what's going to happen, but I just wanted to see if that's OK with you."

Austin shrugs again. "Why wouldn't it be?"

I know he's only five, but my son is smarter than most. When he asks things like this, he's really wondering why it should matter to him.

I sigh and put my arm around his bony shoulders. "Eli isn't your dad, baby," I say, tearing up. I feel a lump in my throat, so I have to clear it before continuing. "I didn't know if you'd feel like he was replacing him."

"Momma," Austin starts, exasperated. "Do *you* like Eli?"

"What?" I'm startled. "What do you mean?"

"Does he give you the spiders inside you? Rosalie makes me get the spiders."

His first crush. He was too young, too innocent to have a first crush. Rosalie. What a pretty name. He isn't wrong, though. I do get the "spiders" inside when I see Eli. I always have.

"He does give me the spiders," I say. "I think it's supposed to be butterflies, though, honey."

Austin giggles. "I know, but spiders are more manly."

My motherly instincts tell me to ask more about this Rosalie character, but I know better. I know who she is and where he met her. I just can't work up the nerve to ask my five-year-old son about the girl he's dreaming about.

"You know you can tell me anything, right?" I tell him, thinking maybe he'll open up more without me having to pry. "I'll never make fun of you or call you names. Promise."

"I know, Momma, but I don't have anything to tell."

Austin has been dreaming about Rosalie for as long as I can remember. Since he started talking, her name has been on his lips. Hers was the second name he learned, after mine. Well, "*Mom*." Who she is and where she comes from, I have no clue. She's a mystery to me. I started dreaming about Eli when I was six, too. I never wanted this for my future children. Yes, Eli was a great person to have in my life, but I never felt normal. I don't want Austin to feel that way. He doesn't deserve the feeling that no matter what he does, he won't be normal.

I wouldn't have felt normal anyway. Even if I'd never met Eli, I'd still be the girl whose parents beat her; the girl who would never fully believe she was loved by anyone because she'd been made to feel like she wasn't worthy of any of it. I would've rather been ignored completely than treated the way I was.

Eli's parents did just that. As long as he wasn't causing trouble, he was in the clear. He hated not having any attention at all; even if he got it from Nanny June, it wasn't the same. I guess we both couldn't win.

"Is Rosalie *your* girlfriend?" I ask Austin now. I don't want to walk around the discussion.

Austin's face immediately looks disgusted, *appalled*, that I would even ask such a question. "No, Momma! Gross."

He finishes his ice cream cone while I look around for Eli. I knew he'll be meeting us here; he told me to come to the bench he bought for June. "*Dedicated to the best mother two boys could ever have.*" I didn't know June had died. Obviously, I wasn't around when it happened, so why would I? It strikes me that we've lost so much time that we'll never get back. I'll always think, "What if?" It'll never stop going around in circles in my head what could've been if we'd run away together, if I'd married him like he asked. I believe he would've married me and been happy with me forever and ever. I just don't think I would've been able to say the same thing.

Eli

Present Day

Hospital monitors beep and air flows through breathing tubes as I look over yet another chart. I have to reread it multiple times; I'm in shock. My body feels numb from the neck down. If I didn't know better, I'd think I'm having a stroke.

"He told us not to tell you," Angela says. "He said he'd fire us."

I snort ironically and nod. "It's not your fault," I tell her. It isn't. No one can change what's happening. The fact that I'm just finding out about my father's illness has nothing to do with anyone but him. Keeping it to himself is a typical thing for him to do, and that's why I'm not upset with anyone else. I won't be surprised if my mother doesn't know either.

"Which room is he in?" I ask, closing the chart file. I ask sarcastically, "Luxury suite, I take it?"

Angela shakes her head and smiles. "He knew there was more of a chance you'd find out that way."

"What an ass," I mutter. "Well, where is he?"

Angela tells me his room number. Room 222. I could walk there with my eyes closed. That's one of the rooms we use for hospice. We want them to be comfortable and happy. That whole hall is for patients who don't have very long left. Knowing my father was down here too... well, there were no words to describe how I was feeling.

My heart is in my throat, more from anger than anything else. Yes, I'm upset that my father is dying, but if he told me when he was first diagnosed, I'd feel better than I do right now.

My father is too young. He has too much to look forward to. I was going to introduce him to Eleanor, to Austin. I want to show him I'm not just a doctor with nothing else going for me. I want to prove to him that I can have both a job and a life with a family.

Selfish. I'm being selfish. I shouldn't be thinking about myself. He matters more right now than my petty feelings. I slow down. I needed to prepare myself and be strong for him and Mother. *219, 220, 221…222.*

✳ ✳ ✳

"Darling, stop that, will you?" Father requests. My mother, panicky and worrisome, keeps fluffing his pillows. It's been a long time since I've been in the same room with both of them; usually it's just my mum. My father and I haven't seen each other often after our last fight.

His face is very pale and thin. He looks so small—he *is* small. By the time I was fifteen, I towered over him. I think it intimidated him; when I started to build muscle, he didn't like how I looked. "You look like you take steroids," he'd say. There was a chance I could beat him senseless.

My mother is sitting as close to my father as the chair will let her. Tubes in his nose help him breathe, and his hair is starting to fall out. Mother is trying to put on a brave face, but I can tell the second she gets home she'll start crying.

"Now, Eli," Father says, gaining my attention, "my will is in the grandfather clock at the office. You're the only one with a key, and you're my beneficiary. I know you'll do what's right with what I have…" He pauses to cough, and I see that my mother is hesitant to fluff his pillows again. She doesn't know what else to do. "You have a smart mind," he adds. "You'll take good care of everything—everyone."

"Dad—"

"Don't. Don't argue with me on this. I'm dying. It is what it is."

My mother gets up and pulls me in for a hug. We don't hug. She's crying so much from his blunt statement that she's soaking my expensive shirt, and I let her. My father stares out the window, making sure not to make eye contact. Tears settle in my eyes, but none come out.

Mother feels bony and small as well; she probably hasn't been eating much. Just then, Angela bustles in, saying she needs to do a checkup. Dad mumbles something about how she was a snitch and how she's lucky he's too tired to yell at her. I suggest to Mum we get something to eat; Dad's pride still won't allow us to stick around.

"I just can't imagine a life without your father," my mum says as we drink our coffee in the family lounge. I asked one of the nurses to order us food, hoping Mum would eat, but I know better than that. I wouldn't be able to either, in her position.

"Mum, why didn't Dad tell me?" I ask. "It's not like this was some shock. We're doctors. We know how life works."

Mum purses her lips and sighs. "That's probably why he didn't tell you. You would've tried so hard to save him. He knew nothing would. He knew you'd blame yourself."

After our last fight, I never thought I'd speak to him again. It was right before Kit left me, and I was having a rough go of it. When I told him I was going to propose, he wouldn't stand for it as I started my medical career. He wanted me to go back to therapy.

I couldn't. No, I wouldn't. Therapy reminded me of a part of myself I didn't want back. I didn't want to be that desperate fool willing to do anything to forget about a girl who broke his heart. Of course, my father didn't understand, because I had never explained to him about Eleanor.

"You know I'll be there for you, right?" I ask Mum, who's picking at her food but not really eating anything. "I can be there for whatever you need."

"What I need is for the two men in my life not to be at odds when one is nearing his end."

I'm taken aback. She's right. No matter whether I forgive him, he deserves to hear me say I do. No one deserves to die thinking their loved ones don't love them.

Eleanor can look back and think better of her parents. In the end they changed; at least she knows they were changed people. My father hasn't. That doesn't mean I don't love him, but dying shouldn't change things, should it? Could I really look him in the eyes and lie to him by telling him I forgive him when I can't? Nothing has changed.

"Did Dad ever tell you he missed me? Or that he felt gutted about the way he talked to me or made me feel? It's been five years."

"That doesn't mean he isn't."

I snort. "You're right. It just means his pride still outweighs his love. That was the reason we never had a relationship. Not because he didn't say sorry." My face heats, and I can tell I'm flushed. He didn't love me enough to tell me he was sick. That's the worst part. "I can't lie. I don't think I can do it."

Mum abruptly gets up from the couch and walks out. I don't follow her; I don't try to ask her to stay, because there's no point. My mother isn't much better. To say she didn't drink everyday would be a lie. I don't think she can recall any favorite memory of me growing up, because she was almost never sober. I'm surprised *she's* not on that hospital bed.

"Eli?" Angela says, pulling me back from endless flashbacks. "Your father is asking for you."

I sigh. "I'll be right there."

There's a feeling in my stomach telling me I *am* going to lie. I know I am. I'll tell him that I love him and that he was forgiven a long time ago, I just didn't know how to tell him. I'll tell him he can leave now knowing we're OK.

The second he passes, it'll be like nothing happened at all, because he won't say anything back, and he won't tell me he loves me too. He'll say thank you and call it a night. Because his pride will get the best of him yet again while I for once compromise mine. It won't change a thing.

I get up from the couch and grab my breakfast sandwich. Pancakes for buns. It's genius. I take deep breaths as I walk back to Room 222. I tell myself there's nothing I can do now and that I need to just put on my ten-year-old face and help my father go peacefully.

At age ten, I would have done anything for Daddy. He was a role model in my life for years, until I saw what was really happening. Ten-year-old Eli would've climbed into the bed with him and told him all the reasons he loved him. Thirty-five-year-old Eli will have to find a way to show his dad that he forgives him.

Even when he doesn't.

Eli

Age 10

Eleanor sat next to me on a Ferris wheel, taking even, steady breaths. Sometimes, she fell asleep in our dreams. It was like she needed to sleep somehow and this was her only escape. Sometimes, I let her. Her head was on my shoulder, and we sat at the top for hours.

I would imagine all types of things to keep myself occupied while she slept. I imagined days and nights over and over at high speed. I watched a movie with the clouds as white screen. She never even stirred.

"El?" I whispered. I could feel myself beginning to wake up; I knew I didn't have long. "Wake up, El."

She groaned as she stretched and yawned. "How long was I asleep for?"

"A couple hours, it felt like. But I'm waking up."

The Ferris wheel rotated until we were at the bottom. Eleanor sat quietly, knowing if I woke up, she would soon after.

"I'm sorry I fell asleep," she said.

I shrugged. "It's OK. It wasn't so bad. I watched a movie."

We got out of the gondola and started walking around the amusement park, which was assembling itself in front of our eyes. Eleanor's eyes sparkled; she had never seen anything like this before. She ran over to a ring-toss booth. I knew it was rigged; my dad had ruined that for me years ago.

Eleanor threw the ring as hard as she could, and I dreamed that it would land right around the neck of the bottle. Bells and whistles went off all around the park. "*WE HAVE A WINNER.*" El jumped up and down, laughing so hard she was crying. I could hear Nanny June calling my name to wake me up.

"El."

She looked and saw me disappearing. Her laughter died, and all I could think was how I wished I could stay with her forever.

"I love you," I told her. It was the first time I'd ever said that to her, and I didn't know what I meant. All I knew was that her eyes looked a little less scared.

* * *

"Eli, honey wake up." Nanny June was shaking me gently. She looked like she had been running laps or baking in the sun—her cheeks were flushed, but I could see tears in her eyes.

My father was at the foot of my bed. He looked like he had been stewing about something, most likely something I'd done. I could see his arms crossed showing that his impatience was growing.

"What's wrong, Dad?" I asked groggily. I rubbed my eyes.

"What's wrong? Did you not even bother to see what time it is?"

My heart began to race as I looked at the clock. It was nine in the morning on a Saturday. For most kids, that wouldn't be an issue. For me, it was. My father had surgeries most Saturday mornings, and my mother was usually too inebriated to take care of me. It was Nanny June's only day off.

I had football practice on Saturday mornings. It gave my dad enough time to get through one surgery and be back in time to pick me up. Almost always, I was stuck there late, because my father was never on time. I didn't even like kicking a ball around, but my father had signed me up at a young age because that's what he'd done as a kid.

Football started at eight sharp. I'd overslept.

"I...Dad, I'm sorry," I stuttered. "I really don't know what happened."

"I know what happened," my dad snapped. "That useless phone we got you didn't have an alarm set because you're incompetent. You should've been thinking about this."

"That's enough, Henry," June said quietly. "That's enough."

"No, it's not. I had to call you and wait until you got here on your day off to watch him because he missed practice. Which pushed back one of my surgeries. Maybe even postponed it entirely. Are you completely dependable in June that you can't get up on your own? Should I look into hiring someone who won't baby you so much?"

"No!" I shouted. My father whipped his head around to look at me like I had no right to say anything. "I just…Nanny June is irreplaceable, Dad. This isn't her fault."

"You're right about that, my son. It's yours. Apologize to June for making her come in on her day off."

I looked at Nanny June, whose face now looked like it was burning. "I'm sorry, Nanny June. I'm sorry I did this."

She said nothing; it wouldn't be polite to my father. She'd keep her mouth shut or she'd lose her job. She and my father had been friends for years, but he wouldn't hesitate to fire her if she made him look like a fool.

"Good. Now I'm leaving. Give me your phone."

I took my phone off my dresser. He snatched it from me and walked out of my room. Nanny June sighed like she'd been holding her breath. "This wasn't your fault, Eli. Your father works you to death all week; you should be allowed to sleep in on the weekends."

I knew that it didn't matter what she said. I still felt responsible that she had to watch me on her day off. A thickness in my throat made it hard to swallow. I feel tears forming in my eyes.

"You're ten, sweetheart."

"'Ten is nearly a man,'" I muttered, quoting my father.

I pulled the blanket off, raced out of my room, and plunged down the staircase to catch up with my father. He was grabbing his briefcase as I bounded toward him. "I'm sorry, Father. I'm so sorry."

I hugged him, and he let me, but he didn't hug me back. My stomach was churning, waiting for him to say something, anything. To let me know it was OK.

"Next time, you won't forget to wake up."

My arms turned to jam, and I let go of him. He walked out the door without another word. An England drizzle was coming down slowly. Nanny June was at the top of the staircase, watching in disbelief. I wiped a tear from my eye and stood up taller. I would not forget to wake up again.

Eli

Age 31

W hen I decided to propose to Kit, my father was the first person I wanted to tell. For some reason, I was still trying to please him. Every day, my calendar had different things on it—go to school, football, study. But it *always* said "**IMPRESS FATHER**" in all caps and bold letters. I was still waiting for him to say, "Well done, son."

Telling him that I was going to be married was the worst mistake of my life. I brought the ring with me to show him, to see if it was big enough. Honestly, I just wanted to show off how much I could afford. To prove that I was making good money. I dressed in his favorite "leisure outfit," nothing less than a nice dress shirt and tie paired with black pants. The tie had pigs on it. My father had a thing for pigs; his mother had given him one when he was a child, and when she died, pigs stuck. He never spoke of her unless it was about the pig.

I got to the house, and the new maid let me in. She looked terrified to be in such a huge home. Compared to home that she lived in, it was a mansion. "He's in his study," the maid said softly, scurrying off to hide somewhere he wouldn't find her to tell her she'd never be as good as June.

I sat down in front of his desk, waiting for him to get off the phone.

"Yeah, go ahead and schedule that for tomorrow evening." He held up his finger to me. "Oh, Marie, stop."

My father had a way with people when he wanted to. Most of the time he didn't, but when it benefited him, he knew how to kiss ass. "It pays the bills," he would say.

As he hung up the phone he said, "What is it, son? I'm scheduling things right now."

I chuckled ironically, taking a breath. "Well, I actually have something important to talk to you about."

Father looked up at me seriously, taking off his glasses and gesturing to me to continue. I took another deep breath, pulling the ring from my pocket. "I'm going to ask Kit to marry me. Wanted to tell you first."

If I ever saw my father shocked, it was then. He was speechless. For a moment, I thought he was proud of me. *This is it*, I thought. This was the moment he would tell me he knew I was worthy of the family name.

He stared at the box in his hand for a moment, eyes wide. Pulling himself out of whatever trance he was in, he set the box down on the table, not even opening it. "Am I supposed to pat you on the back and tell you what a great idea this is? Because I would be lying. I don't lie."

I let out a breath I hadn't known I was holding. I should've known. There would never be anything more than disdain in his words. He would always be slicing my nerves in half with everything he said.

I stood up, snatching the box off the desk. "I don't even know why I came here in the first place."

My loving father laughed out loud, saying, "Neither do I. Marriage is a mistake."

My hand was already on the door handle. It was the only thing keeping me straight. I shouldn't have turned around. I shouldn't have even asked. "What does that mean? What about Mum?"

"Your mother is not the same woman I married, Eli. If you haven't noticed that yet, maybe getting married will work for you. You're obviously oblivious."

My blood was starting to boil; I could feel my face turning a red, but I couldn't let it go. "She's that way *because* of you, you ass. You turned her into that person!"

He just rolled his eyes and smirked.

"What about me, Father?" I pressed. "Was I a mistake?"

That question seemed to stop him. He stared at me. Again, speechless.

The longer I waited for an answer, the more respect I lost for him and for myself. I finally couldn't take it anymore. I shoved the jewelry box in my pocket with one hand and started pulling off the pig tie with the other. I heard it rip, and out of the corner of my eye I could see him flinch. I couldn't stand to look at him anymore.

Throwing the tie on the ground, I tore open the door, feeling a weight lift from my shoulders. I wanted to get out of that place as swiftly as I could, and no one in this empty house would stop me. I heard the maid's shoes on the tile floor as she ran to open the front door, practically tripping over herself.

As I walked to my car, I heard my father shouting to the maid to come pick up the damn tie.

Eli

Present Day

My legs drag as I walk to the park to meet El and her son, seeing my father in the hospital bed having a coughing fit, hearing him tell me where the will is. Telling me how *proud* he is of me. Never have I heard those words escape his lips. Even if they were right there behind them, on his tongue, blocked by his sharp teeth. He wouldn't bend his pride to tell his son that he appreciated who he'd become.

Now that he's near his end, none of it matters. I was so angry when I saw him. I could barely listen to my mum go on about how much she loved him and how we needed to make up before he died.

What makes him so special that he deserves an apology from *me*? The one who's dying should be the one with regrets. I don't have a single reason to say sorry to him or make him feel better about himself before he keels over. I don't feel bad about that. I don't want to feel at all, to be perfectly honest but the feeling still never went away. I couldn't help but feel sorry for him.

There's still a gnawing feeling in my gut that I need to be there with him, holding his hand and listening to him yell at the nurses, or I'll always think "what if?" It just seems like too much. I want more than this. I deserve more than this too.

"Eli, Eli!" I hear Austin shouting for me in the distance. He runs up to me with chocolate stains on his face.

Eleanor is watching him hesitantly, making sure he's safe. She looks at me, smiles. Her red hair flows to just below her shoulders. She's wearing a sundress that shows off all the right curves, paired with sneakers, which is typical for her; she never liked sandals. "What if I need to run away?" she'd say. "Flip-flops will trip me." My eyes don't leave hers once as I walk toward them both.

Austin jumps up, expecting me to catch him; it isn't too difficult to do, even though I don't see it coming. He's still so small. The more I see him, the more he warms up to me, which makes my day feel a little brighter. Seeing him with El makes everything lighter, like it isn't always raining. There's still a sun somewhere.

El can probably tell something is wrong, but she doesn't say anything. Austin is taking up much of my attention. I don't mind. For a second, I don't have to think.

"Hey, baby," she says to her son. "Here's a couple bucks. Why don't you go ask that man for some feed for the ducks, huh? Just stay right in front of me and Eli so we can watch you have fun."

"OK, Momma!" Austin jumps out of my arms, which rips the shoulder of my suit jacket. "Oops! I'm sorry…"

I chuckle. "It's fine, lad. Don't even worry about it."

He runs over to the man I've seen at this park for the last ten years and asks him for some feed. Of course, the man gives Austin a whole bag which cost more than he's paid. Any time I've been here, he always gives children extra. He seems to have a soft spot for them. Austin jumps up and down, thanking him repeatedly. I laugh, and El does too, then looks at me again with worry and gestures to a bench where we can watch Austin.

"You know, you have a perfect child," I say, grabbing her hand. I can't look at her, because I know I'll fall apart, so I watch Austin. "Remember when you said you never wanted to have kids? Because of your parents?"

El smiles painfully. "All of that perfection is from James, though. He didn't get it from me."

"Oh, I don't know about that. You're still pretty perfect."

"Eli," she says softly, "did something happen today?"

I swallow the lump in my throat, taking a deep breath. "My father is dying."

Saying it out loud, acknowledging that it's really happening, is different than just thinking about it. Especially since it's Eleanor. Being with her now, being able to talk to her again, means so much, but I don't think this is a conversation we need to have.

I can feel my heart racing and my breathing becoming shallow. I'm having a panic attack. I've been having them since the last time I saw El—another reason for the therapy—and they come on when big things happen in my life. They won't go away.

"Hey." El rests her hand on my face, pulling it to look at her. "It's OK. Talk to me."

Austin is still feeding the ducks, chasing a few as he goes.

"He, um, his lungs are failing. There's nothing to do. He might not make it through the night."

They were hooking him up to a respirator when I was leaving, which meant he wasn't going to be able to talk much anymore. My mother was hysterical; she couldn't stop crying as they did it. I've seen it happen to other people, but with him, it's different. I *know* him. He gave me life. He made me who I am.

"Why are you here?" she asks. "Why aren't you with him? Your family?"

I pull my hand from hers and stand up abruptly. "Family? I don't have a family, love. We're not a family. Being around them makes me feel like I'm trapped in a lie again."

She sits on the bench with her eyes on her hands. I'm slowly pacing back and forth, keeping my eyes on Austin. He's given up on feeding the ducks; now he's sitting in the grass, pulling it from the ground.

"We could come back with you."

I stop pacing and look at her with wide eyes. "You're not serious."

"Why wouldn't I be? If you need a support system, we can be it. Austin would like to meet him."

I snort, sitting back down. "He'll eat Austin alive as his last meal. Come on."

She shrugs. "It's up to you. I'm just offering. I owe you that much."

Austin skips down the hall with his hands in mine and Eleanor's, wanting us to swing him. His mother told him to be on good behavior, but not too good. Holding his hand is the only thing keeping me grounded; I don't know what to expect. With how fast my father is declining, I'm not sure what I'm walking into.

On the train ride over, I couldn't let go of her hand. She squeezed my hand tight, not missing a beat. I know that it made her anxious, her fight or flight kicking in almost immediately. El stuck it out for me knowing how hard it's going to be for me to watch the life leave my father's eyes. She knows that I am not going to handle this well.

My mother is sitting on the linoleum outside his room, crying. Her eyes are so puffy I don't know how she can see out of them. I wonder if the thought of her thousand-dollar outfit getting dirty has crossed her mind. She wouldn't be doing this unless it was serious. My father's door is closed.

I run over to her, grabbing her hands. "Mum, what's happened?"

She just looks at me, sobbing uncontrollably.

I shake her softly. "What's happened, mum? Talk to me!"

"Eli." Eleanor is behind me now, and her presence calms me somewhat. I give up trying to talk to my mother, it will do nothing but upset her and aggravate me.

I drop her hands in frustration and stand. My legs don't seem to want to move toward his room. Austin finds my hand again. He pulls me to the door.

Taking a deep breath, I open it.

There he is. The man I once found so terrifying and malicious is now lying in silence, watching some old sitcom on the telly and waiting for his end. He looks so much worse than he did just hours ago; I can't believe my eyes. Immediately I'm by his side, sitting in the chair my mother occupied earlier.

"Dad," I choke out. "Dad, I'm here."

He squeezes my hand so hard I can't feel my fingertips. I can't imagine how it feels to not be able to breathe. I have my panic attacks, but to actually lose your breath, to have no air in your lungs—it cripples me that he can't even doing the simple task of breathing. The fear in his mind must be worse than anything he's ever felt before.

Eleanor sits down next to me and sets Austin in her lap. He bounces up and down for a minute, but stops when he notices my father staring at him. Dad's face is puzzled, and when he turns to look at me, he raises his eyebrows as if to say, "That better not be yours."

"This is Eleanor, Dad. The girl you made me go to therapy for."

Another shocked expression.

"This is her son Austin." I look at her, and she's putting on a brave face for me. Letting me tell my father about us can't be easy. "His father passed away when he was just a baby."

My father winces, almost like he's sorry to hear that. Who is this man? He's not the man I saw just hours ago. Maybe it's the painkillers.

"Do you want to read him my book?" El whispers to Austin. He nods, pulling the children's book out of her purse. I shouldn't be surprised that she has it stashed in her bag, but I am.

As Austin reads, I listen, helping him when he needs it. My father actually seems to be paying attention too, acknowledging someone trying to do something nice for him. He lies there with his eyes closed, but every time Austin starts to struggle, his eyes pop open like he wishes he could speak.

Eventually my mother comes back in. She's finally stopped her hysterics. The nurse brings another chair, and we all continue listening to Austin read. There isn't a single word said besides the story. I can hear my own heart beating. A line from Eleanor's children's book says, "The children had a world of their own, no matter the distance between them." I look at her while she looks at Austin and my heart swells.

The whole time Austin reads, my hand never leaves my father's. He holds on for as long as he can, but by the time Austin finishes, his hand has slipped from mine. A few moments later, his monitor flatlines. We knew this moment was coming; we've known our whole lives. You read about it, you see it in the movies, but you never truly know until it's your own blood.

For a fleeting moment, it's like we were always a real family. There's no brokenness, no heartache. Being here for my father made things better for him, and I understand it was what he needed.

My mum isn't crying now; I think she's run out of tears to produce. I think she's feeling what I am: nothing. I can't think about his presence not being in the world anymore. As hateful as he could be, he was legendary in our community. I'm grateful to have Eleanor here with me to hold me while they cover him with a sheet.

Eleanor

Age 31

I remember the sound of church bells. They were painfully loud as I walked into the building with the rest of James' family. Austin cried whenever I tried to put him down, so I had to hold him at all times. Lana was standing next to me, and I could smell the vodka on her breath. I wished I didn't have to be here.

Funerals made me sick.

Dead bodies in caskets, lying there looking like porcelain dolls, made me nauseous. I understood the concept, but I would never like it. Now, having to see my own husband lying there with his face plastered in a straight line was too much to bear.

Thanking people repeatedly for their condolences was also not high on the list of things I wanted to do. I was exhausted. I just wanted to sleep. I'd just done this a few nights ago for my parents, who had wanted to be cremated, thank God. I knew if I could get through James' funeral, everything else wouldn't seem too hard.

After everyone was seated, the preacher started a prayer. Austin couldn't stand me kneeling and rising during the service, and standing too late was not an option. The next thing I remember is grabbing his diaper bag and wandering off to find the nursery.

"Come on, baby," I whispered to him, sitting down in a rocker. "It's OK."

For a moment, he wouldn't stop; he continued to cry for another fifteen minutes before I broke and started to cry with him. It was an intimate moment with my baby, and I realized he wasn't crying to sit or stand or eat or sleep. He wanted his father to hold him and speak to him in that beautiful soft voice.

Not long after, Austin dozed off. I'd already missed most of the service, and I hid in the nursery to avoid having to hear any more apologies. I hid so my son wouldn't wake up to find that his father still wasn't there. I hid because I wanted to; I didn't want to deal with it anymore.

No one would know how I truly felt. Apologies meant nothing. They were just hollowed-out words that were polite to say in a situation like mine. Empty phrases were meant for people with nothing left to hold on to.

Eli

Present Day

I can hear the church bells ringing, but they sound distant. Everything sounds distant as I walk into the hall where my father is waiting for his family to say goodbye. My mother is next to me, John trailing behind with Willow. There aren't many people left I consider family; most of my father's family is dead.

My father's funeral was arranged overnight; so many people in the community loved him that I didn't have to do anything. I found his will right where he said it would be: in the grandfather clock in his study, in a black envelope with my name on it. I knew he had a lot of faith in me. I'll have to make sure it's exactly what he wanted.

A few people helped organize the funeral. My father had a past patient that is a member of the church that we're having the funeral at. They were listed in the will to call and set everything up, they would take care of the rest.

The church we're in is very old and very Catholic, like my father. The entryway is big enough to hold a service outside on a nice day. I would prefer that. The fresh air feels nice and gives me a chance to breathe, but it doesn't help. I still feel like my lungs are filling up with water. I can feel tears start to form.

Mum's not in her right mind. I've known it from the moment I picked her up from the house. As we sat in the cab on the way to the church, she just cried. I can tell she's been doing nothing but crying for the past few days before Father died. She fired the maid because the only reason she had one was my father. Mum doesn't know how to cook, and she's usually too drunk to clean these days.

161

Now, it doesn't matter. She won't need anyone to cook her food or clean her house. She'll let herself starve if I let her. She's already spiraling out of control. I wondered if she's been like this longer than a day.

Eleanor promised to meet me here. She's going to try to find someone to watch Austin—Lana still hasn't come back, which is starting to worry her. She made a couple calls and is waiting to hear back. The sea of sad faces here to pay their last respects to my father makes it hard to try to spot El. I'm not surprised how many people have shown up; he was loved by all he interacted with. They all part silently with pity in their eyes as I make my way to the casket. I have to force myself to approach his corpse, my legs paralyzed.

My father looks pristine as usual. The hair he has left is slicked back, and he wears his favorite suit. It's the same one I'm wearing. He has on his pig tie. We got them together right before I joined his practice. There are two rings on his hand—his wedding ring and his father's. He only took them off for surgeries. Even then, they hung on a chain around his neck.

If I have to say thank you to one more sad individual I don't know, I'm going to scream. My hands are sweaty from all the shaking, or maybe it's just from the stress. My uncle is next to offer his condolences, and he's blubbering. He was always like this growing up; he's worse than my mother. I can't handle him. Not *another* sad person.

"I need a minute," I whisper to John.

I decide to sit on a stone bench with cherubs on the side. My heart feels like it could rip through my suit jacket and land in the rubbish bin next to me. I hold my face in my hands, waiting for the water to drain from my lungs.

"Eli?" I hear Eleanor's voice and look up to find her standing in front of me in the blackest outfit I'm sure she could find on such short notice. It's a long dress with lace sleeves. She looks stunning as usual. Her red hair is in a low bun with strands falling out. She doesn't have any makeup on, which I adore; it makes her more admirable.

I clear my throat before saying, "You look beautiful, love."

Eleanor's pale cheeks turn pink. Tension has been building between us since we kissed the other night. All I can remember is her hands on my face, under my shirt, my lips on her neck, the sound of her breathing. We haven't talked about it or kissed since.

"I've been where you are," she says, sitting down next to me. "The panic attacks. Not being able to breathe."

I chuckle. "Yeah, but you're stronger than I am these days."

Eleanor puts her hand in mine, which I realize is shaking uncontrollably. My palms stop sweating. It's like she's the only person in the world who can get me through this the way I need to get through it: with someone by my side.

"I didn't used to be, though; you know that." She looks at me like she's trying to find a memory buried in my mind. "Do you remember all those times when we were about to wake up and you told me everything was going to be OK? I *did* believe you."

I look at her. I can tell she's serious. "You did? You never..."

"I know. I never told you that before." Her hand is still in mine as she says, "We should probably get you back in there."

The rest of the day she's with me. She doesn't leave my side as long as I need her there. Her hand is in mine during the whole service, while everyone says their nice things. "He saved so many lives." Everyone says that. Everyone mentions what an amazing father he was and how he treated mum with the utmost respect.

My mother sits through the service with a blank face. No one seems to notice but me, and I grab her hand with my free one. She has her wedding ring on; it's cold against my skin. A constant reminder that there's no one keeping that promise to love her and keep her safe anymore. There'll be no one to hold her when she's sick—which he did, believe it or not—and no one to tell her how beautiful she looks.

On our way to the hall for the lunch our driver, Charles, eyes are red. I want to ask him if he's okay, if he needs anything, but from the looks of it that might just make things worse. He mostly drove my father around everywhere. Now he's gone and he has more time on his hands; time he doesn't want. Charles worshiped the ground he walked on.

During lunch, we're all silent. Eleanor gets food for my mother and tells her she needs to eat; she knows how it feels to not have food in her stomach. She spins it in such a way it *does* make my mum eat. I guess that's why she's a successful writer.

"Why don't you have just one bite?" she asks with a soothing voice. "If you can't stand it, I won't ask again."

Eleanor holds up the buttered roll that's sitting on my mother's plate and she grabs it. Before my mother bites into the roll, she looks at El one last time. She nods her head, her eyes reassuring her that she will be okay. When she bites into the roll, it seems like everyone, including Charles lets out a silent breath they've been holding.

Once we all begin eating, everyone becomes more talkative.

"That's John, isn't it?" El leans in to whisper to me. I can feel her breath on my neck, and it sends chills down my spine.

"How'd you know?" I ask, leaning into her as well.

She shrugs. "I don't know. He's here with you, and you've never mentioned any other friends. He's…something."

I chuckle. "He's a bit of a twat, isn't he?"

We both look over at John with shrimp up his nose. What's even funnier is that his wife, Willow, thinks it's hilarious. She's taking pictures to post on her blog so that everyone can make fun of him. John got lucky; he has someone who thinks his dorky, obnoxious ways are more funny than annoying.

"John," I call across the table. He looks at me, shrimp still up his nose. "Come here, mate."

Pulling the food from his orifice, he drags his chair out so far he hits my Aunt Cherry in the back. "Sorry, lad," John says, not realizing she's a woman. I snort. He hasn't changed a bit. Willow apologizes to my aunt, grinning. Eleanor laughs to herself as John walks over, fixing his trousers.

"John, this is El," I say, gesturing toward her. "El, this is John."

John's face changes from slightly wary to shocked. "You're the girl he was all bent out of shape over all those years ago!"

El looks at me with a face I don't quite recognize. It looks almost as if she can't believe he knows about her.

"Well, he never really mentioned ya," he amends. "I didn't know your name, but I could tell that you were somethin' special, because he refused to let me get him laid."

"Oh, OK," Eleanor says, humoring him. "I'm sure that was why."

My face is hot, but if I hadn't introduced them now, John would have done himself later when he was drunk and incoherent. John whistles for Willow to come over, and he introduces her to El as well. "Can you believe someone would want to marry me?" he says. "*Me*, for God's sake."

"You my love, are perfect." Willows says, just loud enough for us all to hear. "My whole world."

He's my best friend, and that's something that will never change, but there's a difference between friendship and love. I think John is one of the most embarrassing people I've ever met, and he knows it. Willow loves him for all he is. Everything about him is just the way she likes it. My mind never could comprehend that.

My mother starts to laugh at John too, which shows me that life is starting to return to her heart. The day is getting away from us, and I know El will have to get back to Austin soon. I'm sure it wasn't easy finding someone to watch him while Lana's gone. It's only been a day or so, but I know soon she'll go from mildly concerned to anxious. After all, James left her to take care of Lana.

"Do you want to get out of here?" I whisper to her, my lips brushing her ear.

Eleanor looks at me, her nose rubbing mine. I can smell the wine on her breath, and her cheeks are flushed, but I can tell she's not drunk— maybe slightly sloshed. She nods yes. "Austin is probably waiting for us."

Us. There's an us, isn't there? We still haven't talked to one another about the subject, but who's had the time?

My car is now waiting out front with my driver nodding off

"Charles," I say, knocking on the half-opened window. "Alright, mate?"

"I—I'm sorry sir, I probably shouldn't drive. I'm a bit plastered."

Charles drove my father around for years—he deserves to mourn too, in any way he knows how. But he isn't going to drive us home.

"It's not a problem, Charles." I put my hand out for the keys. "Give me the keys. I'll drive you home. Believe it or not, my father taught me."

Charles chuckles and hands me the keys.

Eleanor holds my hand while we drive back to her hotel after dropped Charles off. It's strange having someone to lean on. It's been almost four years since Kit and I broke up. Since then, no one has really been around. I had John, but by then he had Willow. They were happy, and my miserable attitude would've brought down the house most days.

She's quiet; she doesn't say much on the drive. I think she knows I'm thinking about the same things. The bright telephone poles and headlights light up her eyes, making it hard to focus on the road. I want to hold her in my arms again and kiss her until the end of my days. When we pull up to the front, the valet takes the keys, and I give a generous tip.

"Do you mind if I walk you up?" I ask.

At this point, it's late. John kept us entertained for hours, but I know that if I don't come up with her, I won't ever get answers. I honestly still don't think I will; I'm downright terrified to ask her if she has feelings for me.

She looks exhausted, so I expected a *no* from her mesmerizing lips. All she does is nod and hold out a hand. I take it.

We have the elevator to ourselves. Let's just say I'm more than tempted to push her up against the mirrored wall and kiss every inch of skin I can find. But I don't. *Coward.*

The elevator dings on her floor, and we get off, her hand never leaving mine. Even as sweaty as mine are, she doesn't let go. If anything, she holds on tighter, as if she expects one of us to wake up. When she pulls out her hotel key, all I can think about is yesterday morning, when Austin pulled out his key, so excited to unlock the door. The hallway is empty as we stand in front of her door. It's past midnight.

That kid is so amazing. He's a perfect match for her. Having her as a mother is probably the best gift he could ask for. I always knew she'd make it to this point, and I don't care anymore that it wasn't with me. I know that it was supposed to happen.

Everyone meets people. We all get to a point in our lives when we can see clearly that this is how it's supposed to be. We were meant to meet the people we met, and we were meant to see the things we saw before we got to where we are now, standing in front of each other once again.

She's about to put the key in the door when I say, "Hey, El?"

When she looks at me, I don't hesitate. I pull her in and kiss her. Her face is still warm from the wine, and when I kiss her deeper, I can taste it on her tongue. She moans softly, backing herself against the door. Her arms wrap around my neck, her fingers tangling in my hair. When she pulls, I can't help but groan against her mouth. Everything inside me is burning; my lips feel like fire.

My hands start to trail Eleanor's curves, and this time she doesn't stop me. She sighs as my hands find her hips and pull her closer. Her legs are covered by her dress, but it doesn't matter. I squeeze her thighs, causing her to bite my lip and then make her way down my jawline to my neck. I hold on to the doorframe so I don't fall over while she makes her way back up to my lips, pulling me back to her.

I can *feel* myself not being able to stop. I can tell that if I continue this, I won't ever tell her the truth. My feelings will never come out in anything but kisses and moans.

I pull away, taking a breath. "El—"

"I'm leaving tomorrow."

I step back for a moment, shaking myself back to reality. "You're what?"

Eleanor's breathing is shaky as she says, "The book tour. I have a reading tomorrow, and then I move on."

Just like that, the moment is over. Just like that, she manages to break my heart all over again with just a few words. It's not like I didn't know about the book tour. I always knew. The last few days have been so bizarre that I completely forgot she wasn't saying here forever. How could she? Her life is still in New York. This isn't permanent.

Her words are, though. They always were. The way I feel for her is permanent. It's a scar on my chest that didn't heal right; it's pain every time my heart beats. It's a constant memory of Eleanor. She's never left my life, no matter how hard I tried with Kit, with my career.

And now that we've finally seen each other in person, now that I've held her and touched her and kissed her lips and been able to remember how it felt, she's going to be impossible to forget. God, I'll have to go back to therapy.

Eleanor grabs my hand, pulling me from my thoughts. She asks, "Do you still want to come in?" There's no hesitation as I follow her into the hotel room one last time.

Eleanor

Age 17

W e should get married," Eli repeated, slower this time so I could understand.

I laughed at him. I must have been dreaming *within* a dream. "You've got to be joking." I sat up, pulling a sheet over me. Having sex with Eli was becoming one of my new favorite pastimes. Half of the time I didn't believe it to be real. We were always asleep when it was happening. Maybe we were just dreaming of sleeping with each other.

For over ten years, Eli had been my one and only best friend. Of course, in the real world, I had other friends, but no one who meant as much to me as Eli did. Sleeping with him was just an added bonus. I didn't think he'd want more than that. My mistake.

"Why would I be joking? You know I love you," he said, pulling me against him. His body was so warm. "You're the only person I've ever truly loved."

He started to slowly kiss my neck, which sent shivers down my spine. He knew what it did to me, and he was using it to his advantage. Eli had a way of using my weaknesses against me, even here in the dreamworld. Outside of it, we barely had any contact at all. He put his hand on my thigh and squeezed.

"Stop." I winced in pain. I had a giant bruise on my inner thigh.

Eli sat up next to me so quickly that I felt a slight breeze. He makes the sheet disappear with his mind, making me self-conscious. I had the urge to cover up my scars. We were in the middle of the woods, lying

169

on a mattress so we could look at the stars. For some reason, it was chilly in this dream.

"When did this happen?" Eli asked, rage filling his face. "When, El?"

My face started to warm as I calculated what kind of lie he would believe. I never had to tell him exactly what happened. He knew my parents hit me. He knew my parents did a lot of things. But we never actually talked about it.

"I don't want to talk about it," I said simply. "It's none of your business."

Our setting changed. That feeling always made me want to throw up. It was like we were going down the rabbit hole, spinning in circles. When the world re-formed around us, we were on a couch in a cabin. We were both fully dressed, and there was a fire on. I turned to Eli and saw that he was wearing a sweater and sweatpants. So was I. It was snowing outside now, and there was a cool breeze coming through the crack under the door. Every time I moved, my ribs hurt.

This time I'd been punished for staying out too late. My parents had told me I needed a job, but now that I had one, they didn't want me out. They stole all my paychecks anyway. They claimed it was for bills, but usually they came home drunk off their asses, kicking and screaming.

How could I tell my best friend that I had to fight to keep things that belonged to me? Eli never had to fight for anything. His life was set up for him. He was going to be a doctor, have a fantastic house, meet someone who would treat him like he deserved. Not some white-trash girl from New York who couldn't even make a decent paycheck and keep it from her drunk parents.

"El…" Eli started. "How is this none of my business?"

"It just isn't!"

Now I'd pissed him off. I could just tell from the sound of his breathing that he was trying not to yell back at me. Eli scratched his head in frustration, taking the time to think about what to say next. He always talked so *sweetly* to me. He had a soft voice that made me feel so vulnerable. The only way to not be was to be mean to him. It scared me that no matter what I did, he still cared for me.

I wanted him to yell at me. I wanted him to tell me how horrible I was. Then maybe all of this wouldn't feel so much like a dream. Maybe then I could stop feeling what I was feeling. I could take a break from Eli, from my parents, from everything. I could run away and never look back.

"This is why I want to marry you," Eli said, sounding frustrated. "It has nothing to do with what I feel for you."

"But you *do* feel something for me," I said, my own frustration mounting. "That's why you're trying to help me so damn much."

"You know you really shouldn't talk to me like that."

"What're you going to do? Hit me?" I asked, standing up and storming toward the door. "It's not worse than I've had."

"Why won't you let me help you?" Eli finally shouted.

"Because I don't need any help." I put my hand on the handle. Was I really going to leave? "I should wake up."

"Eleanor, please don't leave. Please."

I sighed. I couldn't leave him. I didn't have a rotten enough heart. I could wake up any minute—we never knew how long we would have—so I knew I should stay. I turned around to look at him again. I loved to look at him.

Taking a step back toward him, I took off my sweatshirt. I had a light tank top underneath. Eli liked to be practical in our dreams; he was always attentive to the details. He knew how much I liked to cover my body up like there was a secret I was hiding. Usually, I was.

"We don't have to talk anymore," Eli murmured. His breath came out ragged. He gulped. He stood, took my hand and drew me over to the fireplace. "We don't have to talk at all."

I smirked up at him. He towered over me now. "That works for me."

His eyes were locked on mine, taking off his shirt too. He didn't have anything underneath, and I wondered how he got the body he had. I was sure that if I was getting enough food, I wouldn't look so *flat.* He pulled me in roughly, like he was still angry at me. As long as I could block the feelings he gave me, he could pull me however he wanted.

As I fumbled with his pants, he grabbed my face and kissed me so passionately that I couldn't contain myself. As much as he wanted this to work, I knew it wouldn't. We didn't even live in the same country. As long as we had this universe together, I was perfectly content to pretend everything was OK. That was why I didn't want to talk about the bruises. I wanted to pretend things were fine.

While Eli whispered into my hair how much he loved me, I tried to ignore the pain in my ribs.

Eli

Present Day

Listening to El read her book to a bunch of young children is enthralling. She makes everything so believable. The kids hang on her every word. They ooh and aah when she talks about the adventures the children embark on to find each other.

Austin, on the other hand, has heard the story so many times that it bores him. He knows it from front to back. He can recite it, and did on our way to the library for the reading and signing.

Austin tugs my suit jacket impatiently. "You promised we would read something else while Momma reads."

I chuckle. "Of course, lad. Let's go."

Austin takes off down one of the aisles, just slow enough for me to keep an eye on him. He grabs a book from the shelf and sits down in front of it. He's invested; he doesn't stop reading even when I grab a book of my own and sit next to him.

Pretending to read is hard. I manage to listen to El from where we're sitting while Austin follows his finger along the page. He occasionally asks for help with a word, but he does so well on his own that I wonder how Eleanor got so lucky with a boy like him.

"Wow, you're still here, huh?"

I turn my head to see Lana standing over me with sunglasses and her hood up. She looks like she hasn't showered in days; and even from a distance, I can smell her breath, which can only be described as "something died in there."

"Someone had to watch Austin," I say harshly.

173

Lana scoffs and sits down with us, taking up the whole aisle. She starts to bite her fingernails, which have chipped black polish.

"You don't get it. My brother was all I had, and he's gone. It's been years, and I still can't move on."

I can't hear Eleanor reading anymore, which means she's probably signing books now. I'm not going to have a conversation like this in front of Austin; he knows what's wrong with Lana, but that doesn't mean he needs to hear all the things I want to say about her.

"Austin, why don't you go see if your mother is done?" I suggest. He puts down his book, pauses when he sees Lana, then zooms off to find his mom.

"Lana, my father died the day before last. James died four years ago. You need to stop using James as an excuse."

She looks at me with tears in her eyes. Then she sobers up, her eyes growing cold. "I don't have to listen to you about how my life should be lived. You don't even know me."

When she stands up, she kicks the book out of my hands. I don't say anything as she walks away, but I watch her. She makes her way to the exit, past Eleanor, who doesn't notice her. I put Austin's book away along with mine and make my way over to them.

There are a few more people getting their books signed, and Eleanor looks humbled. Austin sighs.

"He gets so bored," Eleanor told me last night. "We've already done America. That's enough time for a five-year-old to tire of things like that. He misses normalcy; he misses being five." She asked me to come with her for the rest of the tour.

"Would you ever consider coming with me?" She asks.

I'm taken back. I never thought I would ever hear her ask me to go with her anywhere. When she started telling me about Austin needing a normal life, I thought that meant she would be going back home for New York where he could start preschool, make friends.

"Come with you?" I repeat, speechless. "Come with you."

"Yes," she says, deadpanned. "But I won't ask again. You have your own life too."

Thinking about putting my life on hold feels reckless. With my father's death, I have a duty to be "next in line." If I leave now, people will think less of me as a doctor. People will drop the practice, and my father's legacy will be retired because of my selfishness.

On the other hand, Eleanor is all I've ever wanted. If she'd asked me to drop everything when we were eighteen, I would've. I would've crossed the ocean for her if she'd asked. There were so many times over the years that I've been tempted to hop on a plane to New York. When we were eighteen, my mind was made up: I loved her and there was no changing that.

Things are different now.

My life *has* to matter. All the years we spent together, I always made sure she was OK and happy. I sacrificed a lot for her just to show her someone cared. There were times I stretched myself paper thin to please her, and she took me for granted. I couldn't let that happen again.

It's not like El does it on purpose; most of the time, I don't think she even realizes it. Even if she does now, it won't matter. If she really loves me, I'll forgive her. I *can* forgive her. I want to. For the rest of my life, I'll make sure we never have to be who we were in our past.

"Lana was just in here?" Eleanor whispers to me, standing up. "Is she OK?"

"Define OK."

She groans, a worried look in her eyes. I realize it doesn't matter if El thinks Lana should stop drinking; it doesn't even matter if she drank herself to death; she'll still be there for her. It's what she did for her parents, and now that she has another family member in distress she'll fall over herself to help.

It all makes sense now. The reason she couldn't love me the way I needed her to was that she was too busy devoting all her energy to people she knew would never love her the way *she* needed them to.

The way she needs to be loved was the same way I needed her to love me. She never got that from her parents, which made it hard for her to let someone else try.

As I think about what to say to her, I hear the library doors slam open and feel a whoosh of air. I see El's face. She looks nervous, too startled to move a muscle. Lana is charging back inside, ready to knock over anyone standing in her way.

Eleanor

Age 18

I could see my breath as Sam and I stood in line to something highly illegal. She was dancing on her feet to keep warm. I wondered what we'd been thinking to wear skirts in the middle of winter. The bouncer was turning people away as the line moved up; the kids in front of us looked defeated. We were next.

"We're going to get kicked out," I whispered, shivering. The scraps Sam called clothes had been a mistake. I wanted to cover myself up in two winter coats and a heated blanket.

"Just relax," Sam said, smiling. "I've done this before here."

The bouncer was reading the IDs of the couple in front of us, being very thorough. My knees were shaking. If there hadn't been an icy wind cutting between my bare legs, maybe I wouldn't have been so damn nervous.

"IDs," the bouncer demanded. Sam and I handed them over. He stared at us for a moment, squinting. "You're *both* of age?"

Sam smiled, "accidentally" letting her jacket fall off her shoulder. "Definitely. And if you believe us, you might be able to steal a dance from me."

The bouncer blushed, which seemed strange, since Sam was so young. I supposed men liked women young. I supposed Sam was just that good at hitting on men.

"Go on in," he said. As if it was a promise, he added, "My shift ends soon."

Sam winked and blew him a kiss.

As we walked in, I could already hear the music vibrating through the floors. I let out a breath I'd been holding in since I'd handed the bouncer my license. My wrist already itched from the band I wore to prove I was allowed to drink. Sam wrapped her arm in mine, squealing. "Aren't you excited?"

"Sure," I lied.

I couldn't remember why I'd agreed to come. My nerves were starting to melt. I could feel the vibration traveling through my body, making me forget about everything else. When we could finally see inside, all I could see was strobe lights and bodies. Sam immediately dragged me to the bar, where we flashed our itchy wrists. She slapped five dollars on the counter, demanding two Rum and Cokes.

The drinks took what seemed like hours. In the meantime, I watched the dance floor. There was the outgoing crowd, the people who got all the attention. People danced around them to see what moves they had.

There were the guys who were desperate enough to be pushovers. It was so typical and easy, I wondered if Sam would do it.

Then there were the guys who stood against the wall waiting for an eligible man or woman to walk in that they could take home with them. That was typical too, but most of them probably got exactly what they wanted.

As Sam handed me my drink, I noticed one of the wall guys staring at her. She didn't seem to notice; she was too busy chugging down her drink, ignoring the straw. As soon as she finished it, she asked the bartender for another. I sipped mine slowly.

"Hey, Sam," I shouted over the music. My heel was sticky from all the spilled alcohol and sugary drinks. "I think that guy is staring at you."

I gestured toward the back wall while Sam swayed her hips to the music. It wasn't something I favored, but I assumed the drunker you got, the more fun you had. The last time I'd drunk was when I was fifteen, at a high school dance, and it hadn't ended well.

I made point of letting Sam know that. But it was my eighteenth birthday, and in her twisted mind, she was doing something nice for me by giving me a fun night out. I couldn't say no to the only person who wanted to spend time with me on my big day.

I'd promised Eli I would be in our dreams tonight so he could see me as a new person. "You'll be a woman," he'd joked. "I want to see if you'll look different." I was sure it was an excuse, but I accepted it.

Sam laughed, looking in the direction of the mysterious guy. "He's not looking at me," she said, rolling her eyes. She almost looked jealous. "He's looking at you, girl." She pushed me gently, causing me to spill my drink on my scrap of clothes. I shot her a pointed look. She just shrugged, taking a sip of something that was different than what I had on my outfit. Setting my drink down on the counter, I tried to wipe some of the alcohol off me. It smelled worse on me than in my cup.

"Do you need help with that?" someone asked behind me. I barely heard him because he wasn't shouting. It was the wall guy.

"No," I shouted. "I'm fine."

I looked around for Sam, hoping to use her as an excuse to walk away from him. She was currently flirting up a wall guy as well, whispering something probably nasty in his ear. When she caught my gaze, she raised her eyebrows, as if saying, "Why not?"

I sighed, wishing I could be anywhere else. For a moment, I even wished I was home, until my brain slapped some sense into me. Anywhere was better than home. The wall guy was still standing next to me, but he looked more interested in getting a drink.

"I could use another drink," I said hesitantly. "If you don't mind."

He looked at me, baffled. "How old are you?"

"Old enough." Something I learned from Sam. "You?"

The bartender brought the drink he ordered, which looked a lot like the one I had spilled all over myself. "Old enough," he said, handing me the drink he ordered. "For you."

"You didn't even know if I'd talk to you again. Why would you buy a drink for me?" I inquired, genuinely curious.

"I don't give up," he said, moving closer to me. I could hear him better now. "You interest me. Watching everyone. I want to get to know you."

My heart skipped a beat as I looked him over. He had glamorous clothes on. A Calvin Klein shirt, Louis Vuitton watch, paired with Armani loafers. He had a lot of money. The watch on his wrist looked like it cost more than my parents' apartment. His hair was perfect, like he'd just had it cut today.

I took the drink from his hands and sipped on it. It was as strong as the last one. I realized it was the bartender's job to get the customers drunk. Ignoring the straw like Sam had, I took two huge gulps, emptying half of it. The wall guy stared at me, amused.

Coughing from the taste, I asked, "Do you have a name?"

"Do you?" he countered, a devilish smile painted on his face.

"I'll tell you my name if you buy me another drink."

He didn't hesitate to throw down more money. My God, how much could you possibly hold in your pockets? I tried to look unimpressed, like his money didn't matter to me. This was another thing I had picked up from Sam.

Handing me another drink, he said, "Well?"

I finished my first and picked up the second. This time, it didn't taste as bad. "Alice. My name is Alice."

Sam had also taught me that telling guys you intended to never see again your real name was a mistake. They could find you if they really wanted to.

"That's a pretty name," he said, moving closer because of the people around us trying to get their drinks.

"Yours?"

"Scott," he said, extending his hand. "Nice to finally meet you."

I giggled. Since when do I giggle? "You too, Scott."

Our faces were too close for strangers, but because of the other strangers, there was nothing else we could do. Scott could tell I was getting uncomfortable, so he grabbed my free hand and asked, "Do you want to join your friend over there?"

Sam now had multiple suitors lining up to give her drinks and serve her. It was like we were in an English court: Sam was the woman of virtue, and the men were waiting on her hand and foot. I scoffed, watching them find any reason to talk to her. One guy even attempted to spill a drink on her, but only succeeded in slopping it all over his own shoes.

"I'd rather not," I said. "Can we dance?"

Scott told me to finish my drink. When I had, he pulled me to the dance floor. Hip-hop filled the room; the bass found its way from my feet up into my chest. My body was warm and loose. I felt so bubbly from the two drinks. I almost trip over my own feet, but Scott caught me, pulling me against him.

With both hands on my hips, he danced with me to the music. I could feel his breath on my neck, but I had my eyes closed. Trying not to think about it, I wrapped my arms around him and pulled him closer.

My mind still raced, wondering what I was doing. "It's your birthday," Sam had said. "Live a little." Living had always been hard. Living meant getting punished. I *always* got punished for having any type of fun. Even if I got good grades, bragging about them even slightly wasn't allowed. That meant I was cheating.

Having a boyfriend or friends meant that I was promiscuous. A love life had never been something I'd considered having. If I had, I'd have to lie to my parents and whoever was unlucky enough to think I was worth a damn. My life was tiring enough without more lies. I didn't have the time. It was hard enough trying to keep Eli out of the picture; my parents were good like that.

My folks had a sixth sense for the slightest form of happiness. They knew when I had better days. Those were the days they were determined to make my life more of a living hell. It took more and more every time. As I got older and stronger, their words stopped hurting me and the beatings were harder for them to attempt because I was rarely home.

Soon, though, I'd be gone. Soon I would get my own apartment and live my own life. I would make sure they couldn't find me—not that they would come looking. The safer I felt, the better. No one needed to know who I was anymore. I could start over.

Realizing now that I was *still* dancing with this beautiful stranger, I asked him to grab me another drink. "Soon I'm going to think you only like me for my money," Scott said in my ear, "Wait for me here so I don't lose you." My veins were pulsing; everything inside me was warm. I smiled at Sam as I walked toward her, and all the men turned to see who'd drawn her attention away from them.

"Are you having fun yet?" she shouted over the music. It all sounded the same now. I couldn't name a single song.

"Yeah, Scott is nice." I looked behind me to see if he was on his way back yet. "Do I have to go home with him now?"

Sam's eyebrows furrowed, and she pushed someone away from her, pulling me toward the bathroom. It took longer than it should've; I couldn't believe the number of people who stopped to see if we needed a drink or if Sam wanted to dance. Once she thought someone was worthy of her time, I was left to my own devises. Someone who looked younger than me, asked to buy me a drink.

"I'm with someone," I lied. It was almost on command like Sam always did.

"Are you sure? You seem pretty alone to me." The boy says, leaning in closer to me.

I smiled at him sarcastically. "Maybe they're in the bathroom. You stay here and I'll check."

I pushed past him, not pausing for a second. I didn't even wait to see his reaction. In the bathroom, it was apparent that it wouldn't get much quieter. Women giggled and took photos; girls puked in the stalls. But it was better than out where the music was almost unbearable.

"What makes you think you have to sleep with him?" Sam asked.

I shrugged. "I figured that's how this worked."

She laughed out loud. "Clubs aren't always for sleeping around." Very carefully she nodded toward the girls taking photos of themselves. "Most of those girls won't go home with anyone. Either they have a boyfriend already or they just broke up with one. They're just out having a good time. Like us."

I smiled and thought about it. No commitment. That was my thing. Places like this were perfect for people like me. I didn't have the time or the energy to waste on trying to hide my life from people. Letting people in, letting them know who my parents were, would be like opening an old wound. Not smart or effective.

"Let's go," I said excitedly, pulling Sam back toward the door. "I want to go have some more fun."

Fighting off all the guys who came up to us on the way back to the wall was fun enough on its own. Maybe it was the alcohol getting to me, or maybe it was the effect of letting go for once, but I was enjoying myself with Sam. Most times, I was always on alert and always checking for any signs of my parents, like they even knew how to find me.

"Alice," Scott sighed as he saw me walking back. "I thought you'd left me."

Sam had already joined her suitors again, and I watched as two of them whispered in her ears.

"Bathroom," I said with a smile on my face. I spotted my drink. "Is that for me?"

This drink was different. It was blue and had an energy drink upside-down in the cup. It was something I had never seen before—not even something my parents would try. I looked at Scott pointedly.

"It's called a Trashcan," Scott shouted, grabbing my hand with his free one and tugging me closer. "It's apparently good."

This time I sipped the drink, just in case it was drugged. I never forgot that rule. Scott seemed trustworthy, but it's better than to drink something from someone when I hadn't watched him buy it. After a few minutes, when I was fine, I drank some more. It was good, and it gave me more energy. Hence the energy drink. My skin felt more heated than it had been the whole night.

Scott and I didn't go back to the dance floor; we stayed on the wall, just talking. Most of the things that came out of my mouth were complete lies. I couldn't tell if he was being honest either. It was better this way. Not knowing what was real made it easier, knowing I'd never see him again.

"So," he started. "How old are you really?"

At that point, I was on my fourth drink, and I knew full well I was drunk. I'd already mentally cut myself off after this one. "I'm eighteen. Just turned."

Scott scoffed, stepping back and evaluating me. "Yeah, right."

"I'd show you my real license, but then you'd know where I lived," I joked, straw in my mouth. "You?"

The music was still loud, but I was getting used to it. My hearing seemed to be improving. Scott said, "I'm twenty-two," and I whistled. How was that possible? I was in shock that a twenty-two-year-old wanted anything to do with me.

"Crazy, right?" I said, moving closer to him. My drink was gone now. "I kind of want to kiss you."

Scott's hand was on the small of my back, pressing me against him. "I dare you."

As I leaned in for the kill, I heard Sam yelling my name. "Eleanor, Eleanor!" I looked over Scott's shoulder to see her waving me over to her. She tapped her wrist like it was time to go, and I was baffled. I glanced down at Scott's very expensive watch. It was almost two in the morning.

"Was she calling you Eleanor?" he asked, chuckling.

"Um, no?" I lied.

"I knew it! You don't look like an Alice." Scott was trying to stop me from leaving so he could learn more about me, but I knew that I had to leave. Sam's parents weren't that generous.

"Eleanor, let's go." Sam was next to me now, pulling me away. Her hand slipped into mine. Scott tried to push through the crowd after us. Sam was more persistent and didn't mind bulldozing through people.

"You don't look like a Scott either!" I shouted, rushing out the front door with Sam, leaving him in the dust.

As we ran down the street laughing, my heels in hand. A last glance over my shoulder showed Scott in the doorway, smiling back at me.

✳ ✳ ✳

"He was all like, 'You don't look like an Alice!' And I was just like 'Uh…' like a complete idiot!"

Sam and I were laughing on her bedroom floor. There was popcorn, cereal, and soda all around the room. My head was still spinning from the alcohol, but I was still having a good night. It was one of the best birthdays I'd ever had, and Sam was to thank for that. Usually these things backfired for us both.

"Did you have fun though?" Sam asked, throwing popcorn at me. "I got a few guys' numbers. I'll probably call them in a few years."

I laughed at her and threw some cereal back at her. "Yeah, I wish—" I stopped myself, knowing I'd been about to mention Eli. I'd never been this close to spilling it before. "Never mind."

"No, no, no. Tell me, Eleanor!"

Sam's blond hair was cut into a long bob that stayed curly all the time. Right now, she had it up in a bun with pieces falling out everywhere. She still looked perfect, even in Tinkerbell pajamas. I shook my head and stayed silent, debating whether to lie.

"Come on," Sam said. "You never tell me anything!"

"Well," I started, taking a deep breath. "There *is* this guy. I kind of wished he could be with me tonight."

She squealed loudly, hurting my ears. "Oh my god. For how long?"

I winced as she peppered my with questions, but they were harmless for now. "Since I was little. He doesn't live around here, so I don't see him, like, ever. I think he's in love with me, but I don't think I've ever felt exactly the same way."

"Did you sleep with him?"

I looked at Sam, shocked. How was it so easy for her to bring something like that up in conversation? She did it often and it was usually in the worst circumstances.

"You *did*!"

"Sam, I don't want to talk about him! I'm drunk."

"Which means you *want* to talk about him." She pushed me lightly, causing me to topple over onto the floor. Giggling hysterically, she joined me there. I took a deep breath and closed my eyes. Eli was there, smiling at me with his giant grin.

"His name is Eli. We met when I was, like, six." The words came out of my mouth before my brain could stop them. Definitely drunk, I thought. "I think I love him."

"Ohmygod," Sam said. She tried to sit up on her knees, but teetered. "OK, so, like, does he know?"

"I don't know. I haven't made it easy for him," I admitted, knowing full well that Eli was in love with me and that I couldn't seem to tell him the truth. I knew I would end up losing him.

We talked about Eli for a while; I told her minor things. Sam accepted my answers because it was more than I'd ever given her before. I was vague, but she was happy with the secrets I spilled.

After what seemed like ages, she finally changed the subject, and the tension inside me released. Even drunk, I couldn't seem to let go of the feeling that I was insane. That everything I'd dreamed about was a lie. Traumatic experience.

My mother had told me, in her drunken state, that when I was a baby, she'd let me cry and cry and cry. Some days, she punished me by not feeding me. She told me these things right after I'd been punished, to let me know that she would *always* have control over me. She was the only reason I was alive.

When I thought about it too much, I thought Eli could've been someone I thought up to get through it all. Maybe six was just the first memory I had of Eli because that was the first time I'd tried to cope with the life I lived.

There were so many reasons I never wanted to tell anyone the truth. I knew how it would sound. I knew people would think I was crazy. Either that or they'd want to run tests on me. Or both. I knew they would try to find Eli; they would make both our lives a living hell. Maybe I was just paranoid. Maybe I was so scared to give any affection that I'd started making up scenarios in my head.

Sam fell asleep first, which was usually how it went. My mind kept me up most of the night, my imagination ranging from dandelion fields to fiery graves dug especially for me and my frozen heart that would someday stop beating. Maybe then it would thaw out enough for me to love someone.

Eli

Age 21

D o you think you'll get in?" I asked Eleanor as we picked grass in a football field. We were acting like children for fun, she said.

We hadn't dreamed in weeks, months even. It drained us, and my mind needed to be focused on university. My father had been cracking the whip lately, making sure I was getting to sleep on time and getting all my studies done before anything else.

It was finally holiday break, and I hadn't hesitated before emailing El to ask if she wanted to meet. It took her a while, but she got back to me. She had moved out of her parents' apartment and found her own as far away from them as she could get without leaving the city. She still had the same job as before, at some fast-food restaurant she was working tirelessly to escape.

She was trying to get into college.

"I mean, probably not," she said, ripping out grass from my side of the field. "I don't have any money, even if I did."

I had offered so many times to pay for things. I could get her a phone, help pay for groceries, and more. I could even help her pay for college. She wouldn't accept it. Her pride was all she had left.

I wondered what it would be like if she did get into college. She was a little late, but not by much. Plenty of people went to college late anyway, and I was proud of her for trying.

But I didn't want her to find the wrong guys. A lot of them would influence her in the wrong way. Now that she was free from her parents and didn't have to hide from anyone, I could imagine what experiences she would want to try. I knew how it was and how guys were. I was one of them now. Hitting on girls was starting to become a specialty of mine; El and I had come to an agreement to only sleep with each other when we really needed to.

"Do you think you'll try to date while you're there?"

Eleanor scoffed. "Of course not. Well, maybe."

I grimaced and she noticed. Her eyebrows rose in question.

"They're going to take advantage of you," I started, swallowing the fear in my throat. "I don't want anything to happen to you."

"I'll be fine, Eli. This is all hypothetical anyway." Her tone was high-pitched. She sounded like she was hiding something from me.

I nodded and dropped it, but I didn't stop thinking about it. I couldn't get over the way she said she would be fine. We were definitely nothing more than friends now, but my heart always held a soft spot for her. I would never get over her. She was the one person in my life I'd never thought I'd lose. She was the only person I was afraid of losing.

My father once told me to never let anyone get into my head. He told me that love was weakness and I was better off on my own. I was twelve. How can you *not* let someone get into your head when that's the only place they live? Besides the occasional email back and forth, Eleanor and I only had our minds. There was nothing else to go off.

That was what screwed me the most: she would never get out of my head. I woke in the middle of the night from nightmares of losing her. She wasn't really there, but I still saw her. I saw our life flash in front of me, and every time, I lost her.

"Hey." She pulled my attention from the anxiety that was running around in my mind. "Can we make out for a bit?"

I chuckled at her question. "When do I say no?"

"When you want to be romantic and gross," Eleanor said, pushing me down in the grass, nuzzling my neck. "I love how you never give up on that."

My breathing was shallow as she rubbed her hands on my thighs. "Yeah, well, I'm hopeless."

We stopped talking, and Eleanor had another unromantic night with me. After a while, my mind shut down the hope of ever being with her physically, in real life, no dreaming. I told myself this was my life now that I would always love someone who may never be mine. Even if I wanted to let her go, she wouldn't let me. She'd always be in my mind. Even in darkness, I could still see her emerald eyes glowing.

Eleanor

Present Day

Austin sighs next to me as I sign the last book. Eli is walking this way. He has on a button-down short-sleeved shirt tucked into black pinstriped slacks, traveling down legs that go on for days. He towers over me more than I like to admit. I wonder exactly what Lana could've said to him. I saw her come in. She got here in the beginning, as I was reading a passage Austin was tired of hearing. He could've memorized it if he wanted to; I wouldn't be surprised if he already had.

I wish I could do more for him. In the long run, this tour *is* for him. I'm trying to do the best I can to provide for him, and this is the way to do it. I know he's uncomfortable. He gets impatient listening to the same things over and over. That's why I brought Lana. She joined us not long into the tour so that he'd have someone to spend time with while I did business-related things.

Lana came along for her own benefit too. I wanted to keep an eye on her. James's parents had already started to worry, but the person to wake me up to the problem was Henry, their younger brother. He called me late one night, telling me that Lana had crashed at his dorm and he wasn't sure how she'd gotten there. He went to school two hundred miles from the city.

When he called, my heart dropped. I thought something else had happened; I thought someone else had died. It was then I knew I had to help her, distract her from herself. It did help. For a while. But anytime Austin talked about his father, she became a different person. She became someone we didn't know completely.

And then the drinking started.

"Lana was just in here?" I ask, standing up. My ass is numb from the chair. "Is she OK?"

Eli looks grave. "Define OK."

I groan. I worry so much about her it makes me sick to my stomach. Lana knows that, too, and I think she takes advantage of me. I let her more than I like to admit. The drunken nights when she comes back to the hotel with a stranger—or more than one—or new tattoos or sometimes even a battered face make me wonder why I haven't told her how I feel. She doesn't get to treat me this way. She doesn't get to throw her life away for the sake of her dead brother. No one is winning here.

Before I have time to reply to Eli, the back doors to the library slam open. I turn around at the same time as Eli, and immediately wish I hadn't. Lana storms toward me, and it's hard not to picture smoke coming from her ears. Her face is beet-red with anger. Her fists are clenched into balls of fury.

Being abused, you learn to prepare yourself for anything. My immediate instinct is to run very far away from her. I'm not alone and I can't just run away from every problem that I'm faced with. That was the old Eleanor. Eli and Austin need to see who I am now. They just don't deserve her wrath. This isn't the first time I've felt it, but it definitely doesn't seem the same.

"Eli, can you take Austin somewhere that's not here?" I ask softly, so as to not scare my son, who already looks like he wants to hide under a desk.

"I don't want to leave you alone, love. She could hurt you."

"It was not a request," I say, glaring up at him. My son will always come first. He will *not* get stuck in the middle of a battle of who-loved-James-more.

Eli nods, taking Austin's hand and pulling him away. Lana is staggering, so it takes her a long time to get to me. When she's close enough for me to smell the alcohol on her breath, she pauses. She takes a breath. Her clothes are the same ones she left the hotel in. There are stains I'm glad not to have to identify.

"What the hell is wrong with you?" Lana shouts. Her voice is garbled, and I can see tears in her eyes. "How could you?"

For a moment, I think about being calm. I think about not saying what I need to say. My face feels pink from embarrassment; my knees are shaking. I scoff, thinking about all the times she made being her sister-in-law exhausting. "Me? What about you? You have no right to accuse me of anything until you look at yourself."

Lana's hands are still in iron fists. At any moment, she could whack me upside the head. She wouldn't expect me to see it coming. But I would. I *always* expect that. Even from Eli. It's a reaction that will never go away. I won't let it. I need to keep my guard up at all times.

"You're *literally* screwing someone else. James dies, and you screw someone else!"

The breath escapes my lungs and hangs in the air around us. It takes its time to come back to me, giving me time to choose my next words wisely. The fact that she thinks I'm sleeping with Eli shows exactly how little she knows about me now.

"I just don't understand it," she says. "How could you ever want to be with anyone but him? He was the best big brother anyone could ask for."

I take a deep breath. "Lana, he's been gone for nearly five years. He would slap me upside the head for *not* finding happiness with someone else."

"*No*, you don't get to do that. He's dead. You don't know what he wants."

"But you do, right? I didn't marry him or anything. I didn't *give birth to his child*. I know who he was and what he wanted. Don't you dare tell me I didn't know him."

This conversation isn't going to get better, and I know it. My stomach hurts from the stress, and I don't want to cause a scene in a public library. It looks like Eli grabbed my things as he took Austin out of the building. I turn to leave, wanting to end this argument as quickly as possible. My legs feel like paper; I find it hard to move anywhere fast, but I'm quick enough to get out of Lana's grasp.

Austin is jumping in a rain puddle when I come outside, and Eli is on the phone watching him. A sense of relief washes over me. I start walking down the library steps when I hear Lana shout, "I'm not done with you!"

The pain in my stomach is back, and I turn. "I'm done with *you*, Lana. Get sober and then we'll talk as adults."

"What makes you think I want to sober up, huh? I like it better this way."

"Clearly," I observe. "You haven't had a sober day since James died. It's nice to know you're keeping *my* family's tradition alive."

Eli is off the phone now and on high alert. His hands are in his pockets.

Eli's face screams worry, but I don't want mine to say the same.

"You think you're perfect? You think you can just act like you've never had bad days? My brother is dead."

"My *husband* is dead!" I shout at her. Lana is still standing at the top of the steps. She looks shocked, like she didn't expect me to shout at her. Slowly, so as to not scare her, like she was a wild animal I'm trying to tame, I climb the steps. "You have every right to be upset, but I lost my husband too. My heart will *never* heal from that loss."

Lana still has a cold look in her eye as she says, "Yeah, sure. It seems like that now with Mr. Richy-Rich over there keeping you company. What is he to you? Are you going to get married? Give Austin siblings? Get real. You're just as screwed up as I am, and you know it. You just chose to be that way sober."

It's like she spat in my face and knocked the air from my lungs all over again. It doesn't matter what I say. Lana is never going to forgive me for moving on. She shoves past me. My heart aches as she descends, but I don't turn around to stop her. My feet feel like they're in quicksand; I won't ever be able to move.

"El?" Eli is next to me, his hand on the small of my back. "All right, love?"

Throat dry, I nod but refuse to look at him. I just can't right now. Austin is the one I need. I turn away from Eli, heading down the steps toward my son, who's now sitting in the puddle of water, splashing about. James would've said something like, "He's definitely *your* kid."

When I get close enough for him to notice me, he grins widely, jumps up from the puddle, and runs toward me. He envelopes me in a hug so tight it takes my breath away. It's a good kind of loss of breath, the kind you get when you only have good news. My clothes soak through, and I can tell he's itching to take a nap; his eyes are heavy.

"Let's go back to the hotel, baby," I say, and Eli trails behind us.

* * *

"You know," Eli starts, "by the time you leave, I'll probably know the whole staff of the hotel."

I stare at myself in the mirror on the elevator wall, emotionless. My eyes look glazed. I feel like I'm going to throw up, but then I squeeze Austin's hand and he squeezes back. It helps more than I could ever tell him. It keeps me level-headed. I try to swallow, but my throat is still too dry. I can't even try to speak until I get water into my system.

Am I really being so selfish? Being with Eli—is that wrong? Could I be hurting Austin by dating someone so soon? My life is already such a mess with Lana in it. Can I even attempt to be with someone else? That isn't something I was good at until Eli came back around. I keep telling myself that's why it's OK. He makes everything *feel* OK.

The elevator dings and we're on our floor. Eli's hand finds its way into my free one; Austin still has the other. He pulls us quickly toward the room, which is all the way down the hall. The hall seems to go on for a long time today, and I don't want to run. Austin lets go of my hand, leaving it cold. I felt a little emptier without his touch.

Eli squeezes my other hand, drawing my attention toward him. He pulls it up to his lips and kisses it gently. The heat radiates there and slowly spreads through my whole body, thawing me just enough to give him a tight smile.

"Do you want to talk about it?" Eli asks as Austin swipes the key.

I sigh. "Not particularly. Not at the moment."

Inside, Austin jumps on the bed, which means he'll be asleep within the hour. He makes sure to take off his light-up shoes, which continue to blink on the floor. I take off my jacket and make my way to the couch. It's the only place I feel like I can sit up straight and not collapse with exhaustion.

Of course, Eli follows me. And I don't mind; I like him near me. He is almost like a safety blanket waiting to cover me up tightly if I need him to. As if he knows, he fetches a glass of water that I very much need.

"I'm sorry for how Lana was," I say, finally feeling ready. "She really has changed so much."

Eli shrugs. "I know this can't be easy for you. I'm sure it brings back a lot of bad memories."

He means my parents. It does. It scares me that she tries to use the same tactics to force me to listen or let her do what she wants. I think about that a lot. It's a fear in the back of my mind every day that she might cause Austin physical pain.

"Eleanor." Eli grabs my hand. "Lana said—I mean, she said all those things. Do you believe it? Do you really think we can't make this work?"

I shift uncomfortably. It's not the first thought on my mind. Lana leaving, running off to do God knows what, makes me worry the most. Figuring out the logistics of my relationship with Eli isn't top of my list.

In my head, it won't work. All the ways it could go wrong circle around and around. Eli would say that I only need to think of one way for it to work and it's worth it. But *is* it? Can I put Austin through the loss of another father figure in his life? He doesn't remember his dad, but I know that even as young as he is, he wishes he could.

My son always has to be my top priority. If Eli comes back permanently, will he be the only thing I worry about? Even in the last few days, my mind has been consumed with wondering what he's thinking about. Whether he's thinking about me. If he's detached—just wanting this fleeting moment and nothing more. His dad *died* a few days ago. That doesn't just go away. He's hiding the pain, but it's still there.

"El?" Eli pulls me from my thoughts, squeezing the hand he's holding.

I clear my throat, but it doesn't help. Every word I think of saying gets stuck on my tongue. No matter how I look at it, it just seems wrong. The feelings, thinking into the future. It seems like we'll always come up short. Will I move away from my home and change my whole life to be with Eli? Pull Austin away from the very few friends he has? Or will Eli leave his home, his mother, his friends, to be with me and a son who isn't his? How can I ask him to do that when his mother is still in mourning and he owns his father's private practice?

"Do *you* think it would work?" I ask him as I pull my hand out of his, feeling cold.

Eli scoffs, staring at me. His face screws up in a way I've never seen before. He isn't sad or frustrated; he just looks angry. He stands up without a word, loosening the tie around his now very red neck. I notice how his stubble is growing as he rubs his face, trying to calm himself. I try not to show it, but I'm terrified. He's going to walk away and leave me. He's going to make the decision easier for me.

"Eleanor Scott," Eli murmurs after four minutes which seem like four hours, "I have always thought that this would work. If I was a gambler, I would've bet on us every time. Even knowing that I would lose you again."

My heart contracts in my chest, making it hard to breathe. He's never actually gone there. He's never actually said "You keep leaving me" before. I know it in my heart. I know that I'm the one who ruins things. I have reasons he doesn't understand, but I've never given him an explanation. I make it impossible for him to learn the real me—that little girl who still needs someone.

"Eli, I—I—" I stutter, trying to muster something to explain myself. I have nothing. My lungs don't want to function. My throat is still dry.

"I get it, love," Eli says. He's leaning against a wall now, just watching me. "There's always a reason. Always, without fail. You will choose something over me every time, and I will let you. Because you're you. Because I can't let you go. I never could. I know the outcome, and I won't walk away. I can't. So please. Save your breath. I don't need to hear it. Again."

If I'm supposed to be hurt, then mission accomplished. More than anything, I'm angry now too. I understand why he's hurt and upset. But what about me? I didn't get to defend myself. I didn't get a chance to speak.

"That's it, right there," I start, pushing myself off the couch. "That's why I always push you away. That's why I never want to fight for you."

"Me? What the hell did I do?"

"You act like such a martyr! You sit there on your high horse like you've done nothing but be good to me. Like you've never done anything wrong."

"I *haven't* done anything wrong!" Eli raises his voice, and I think of Austin napping in his hotel bed in the room right next to us. The walls are not that thick.

I shush Eli, nodding to the door. As I open it, I hesitate, wondering if I really want to walk out the door with him. Do I want to fight? Do I want to try to make him understand? Is it worth it? Will I just end up broken and alone again? I can't think of anything worse.

Eli is walking out the door, cursing under his breath, when I say, "Wait."

He stops in his tracks. I step out and shut the door behind me. Now we're in the hallway. Nearby, a maid is cleaning a room. The vacuum is running, so she won't be able to hear us argue.

"I needed you to back off. I needed you to give me space to figure things out, and you couldn't. The more I wanted space, the more you kept suffocating me. I couldn't *breathe*, Eli."

Standing on the opposite side of the hall, Eli refuses to look at me. His jaw is tense, and he takes a deep breath, but he still doesn't say anything. I can feel the air being sucked out of the hallway as we try to gather up our emotions and thoughts just to spill them out again.

"I know that's not what you were expecting, but what *did* you expect from me?" I ask, a lump forming in my throat. "I was an abused little girl. Then a teenager with trust issues. Then a young adult wishing she could start over with no reminders of the past. You were part of that past, whether you liked it or not."

I see a tear fall from one of Eli's eyes, and he quickly wipes it away, trying to prove he can handle hearing this. But it brings up emotions he hasn't been dealing with either. We both know that. From the look on his face, I know he understands but wishes he didn't. He knows I'm telling the truth.

"Love, I never meant to make you feel that way." He sniffles. "I feel like every time I tried to be there, I was pushed away. From the beginning. You made it so hard to read you. I never knew what you were feeling. I never knew if something was wrong. If it was me…"

"It was you sometimes," I state truthfully. Eli winces. "I'm sorry, but it's true. When I asked you to drop something and you wouldn't, it didn't help. It made me feel worse. Sometimes I needed to *not* think about my life. I was with you every few days, months. I wanted to not think about my parents or the pain I felt in my body."

He shook his head, scowling. "I knew that, El. I did. When we were young, it was OK. I dropped it every time. Most of the time, it was because I didn't know any better, but as we grew up and you still wanted to 'forget' about your life, *I* was the one being used. Whether it was to be a human punching bag or someone to screw, I was there for you whatever you needed.

"I fell in love with you, despite all of it. That's not your fault, and I'm not blaming you. It wouldn't be fair to say it's your fault for being an amazing person. But you knew. You knew I was in love with you. I told you, over and over. You let me love you, and you let me in enough to keep me around for you to run to and away from. I know you had a screwed-up life, love. I know that.

"When I told you I loved you, it wasn't to keep you around or because I was afraid of losing you. It was real, and I believed it. You were shut off to me most of the time, but when some light showed through the cracks, I couldn't seem to let *that* girl go. The girl I met in Central Park. With her blue dress and fiery red hair. I loved *her*."

"But that wasn't me anymore!" I exclaim. "I stopped being that girl the second I realized my parents weren't sick. That they weren't hurt or in pain. They were alcoholics, and they took their anger out on me. *Me*. Their seven-year-old daughter. And you were trying so hard to bring back a girl who died a long time ago."

Eli starts pacing up and down the hall. He keeps rubbing his face, stopping to look at me, pacing again. He clenches and unclenches his fists. He sighs repeatedly. I can feel my hands shaking at my sides, so I cross my arms to hold them still while Eli thinks.

I've never told him those things before. I never wanted to fight. I pushed feelings so far back into my mind they were squished behind the walls I'd built up. It's been years since I've even thought about my feelings for Eli. The good, the bad and the ugly. They've been squished.

"Couldn't you have told me that?" Eli asks. "I mean, I know I was an ass sometimes, but I still deserved to know. I deserved to know you didn't love me. I could've moved on."

I sigh shallowly. Here it comes. The big question.

"Why didn't you just tell me that?"

My face starts to feel hot, and I can feel the tears forming. They blind me, making it hard to see Eli's face. I wipe them away, wishing I *could* be that six-year-old girl who wasn't afraid of anything or anybody.

"I was afraid I would lose you. I...I was going to lose my best friend. You were all I had for such a long time, Eli. You were all I needed. I thought I was going to lose you and be alone again. I had Sam, I know. But she wasn't you. I thought if I told you I was too screwed up to be with you, you'd never want to see me again."

I hear him suck in a deep breath. "Eleanor...I...I wouldn't have left you. I couldn't. Everything you were going through...If I had left you, you wouldn't have wanted me anyway. That's a dick move."

I chuckle, wiping away more tears. "You could've dated someone else."

Eli laughs, coming over to stand next to me. His arm is touching mine, and I can feel the electricity bouncing off him. "Yes. I probably would've had a normal teenage experience, too."

"But you would've still loved me? Would still have held a torch for me?" I ask, turning to him and leaning against the wall.

"I don't know, really. I didn't ever try."

"Do you want to still try? To date other people?"

My heart is pounding so hard I think he can hear it. I try to breathe evenly. The answer scares me. After telling him the truth, who knows? Maybe he's changed his mind. I can't blame him for that.

"I tried dating, love. It wasn't for me," Eli says, smirking. "Trust me, I broke a lot of hearts."

"You still want me?"

"I've always wanted you."

Eleanor

Age 21

Waking up, I felt something wet on my face. My room was dark, and at first I couldn't figure out where it was coming from. My eyes, I realized. I was crying. I knew why. I wouldn't be with Eli anymore. I'd told him I'd still want to be around, that I would still want to meet with him sometimes. The bitter truth was that I wasn't planning to. I didn't want to. It was becoming too much for my life. For me. I was starting community college and living on a salary that wouldn't even cover a full month of rent, which meant two jobs and no sleep. Eli had better things to do with his life than wait around for me. For someone who wasn't waiting for him.

There was nothing he could do to change that. I needed to get my life together before I'd have even a slight chance at a real relationship, and if I kept Eli around, I would never have that. With him or anyone else. It would be good for him to get out there and find what he really wanted. All he knew was me. I couldn't have that on my conscience.

It was one on a Saturday morning, and I could hear my cell phone vibrating on my nightstand. Sam. She had started college at New York Institute of Art & Design, which she gloriously yapped about twenty-four seven. Her parents paid for her because she was "the favorite." Her new boyfriend's name was Trevor, and he was in school for videography. "Sam is my muse," he said. He brought his camera with him everywhere and recorded everything she—*we*—did.

"Yo, hoe," Sam shouted through the phone. I could hear the bass bumping on the other end, inviting me to join the party. "What are you doing?"

"Well," I started. Did I want to go out? Wasn't that the point of ending things with Eli? "I *was* sleeping."

"Sleeping? It's only one in the morning!"

If Sam could only see me rolling my eyes…

"Come to my dorm. We're partying. Trevor is doing a cool video."

Taking a deep breath, I mulled it over. I hadn't been to a party in a while. I'd actually been avoiding Sam and her trendy life and trendy boyfriend. I was jealous, but it wasn't just that. I'd been trying to figure out what to do with Eli and where my life separated from him. He hated Sam. He hated the idea that I was out at parties where there were other men. He hated that he couldn't be there with me. That I didn't *want* him there with me.

I had fun with Sam. I did. I could handle myself. I knew my limits. My parents' drinking problem didn't seem to have been passed down. With everything I'd been through, the likelihood of becoming an alcoholic was slim. I knew that bothered Eli too. He thought if I was out with Sam, she would pressure me into getting drunk. He probably thought I'd end up like my parents but didn't want to say so.

"I could make an appearance, I suppose," I said, stretching my legs before getting out of bed.

Sam squealed through the phone. "You will not regret this, I promise!"

She hung up, and I got ready to go. It'd been three years since I'd moved out of my parents' apartment. I hadn't seen them since. I'd made sure to pack the few things I owned on a night they were too trashed to notice. I'd made sure they were barely breathing when I left. I didn't leave a note. I didn't leave any trace.

Sam was in her dorm hallway with Trevor, and he was holding his camera while she talked to some blond girl with a short black dress on. Sam claimed to have slowly realized she was bi. She said she liked to "experiment," which was what she was doing now. Blondie looked shy, like she wasn't sure how she felt about a video camera being shoved in her face. Trevor was inches away from her as Sam leaned in, probably whispering things in her ear. She blushed and turned away but didn't move. Blondie liked what Sam had to say.

As soon as Sam noticed me, she pushed past Trevor, squealing again. "I'm so glad you're here!" she yelled over the music. She was very drunk.

"Where's the alcohol?" I asked, shifting in place.

"Oh! I have a stash in my dorm. I don't trust anyone here. I refuse to drink something someone else offers me," she said nonchalantly, like she'd never taken a blind drink from someone before.

When we got to her dorm room, her roommate was there making out with her boyfriend. The rooms weren't that big, and I couldn't imagine being in close quarters with someone else. That was why I had an apartment. It made some things harder and others easier.

Sam poured me a drink while she talked. "I'm really glad you came. I missed you. You look so cute!"

I looked down. A jean skirt with Converses was my go-to, but tonight I'd decided to change it up. Different me. Someone no one knew. I'd chosen a strappy light-blue sundress that hugged my curves, or lack thereof. Sam had bought it for me one night after a party. It was 6 a.m. and we hadn't slept, and she'd wanted to get me something cute. She probably didn't remember. My sandals matched the dress, which, according to Sam, was a fashion-forward look.

Outside, I'd been cold; it was mid-September, so the air was sometimes chilly. The hall, though, was stuffy and loud. There was no room to *feel* cold. A few people looked at me as I came inside. I could feel it, though I refused to make eye contact.

I was used to being stared at. Most of my life, I'd thought it was because of the busted lip or the bruised cheek. "It's because you're hot," Sam told me. She always told me I should embrace it. Embrace the "hotness." I, for one, did not see that, but maybe that was just my screwed-up mental state.

"Thanks," I told Sam, taking the drink she poured from me. "So what's the video about?"

Sam took a big gulp of her drink before talking. "Oh my God, it's so cool!"

She went on to tell me that Trevor had a vision—he wanted to make a documentary on college life and what it meant to find yourself in such a big city with so many people.

"How original," I said sarcastically. During the conversation, I'd downed my terrible-tasting drink to try to find some amusement in Trevor's vision. I was buzzed. "Did he start it already?"

Sam looked behind me and smiled from ear to ear. "Ask him yourself!"

I turned around to find Trevor holding his camera in my face like this was a zoo or something. Like I had no right to what was shot of me. Like he could publish anything he wanted.

"Trevor," I started, looking directly into the lens, "if you keep shoving that thing in my face, I will break yours and your camera."

Trevor put the camera down and scoffed. "You'd owe me a new one."

I laughed, feeling the alcohol in my veins. Sam poured me another cup as she listened to us bicker. She liked the drama because she knew it was harmless, and she liked that I was making conversation with one of her many boyfriends. I didn't like Trevor, but Trevor debated with me all the time, which was better than the boyfriends who wouldn't even look at me.

"Oh, so your daddy won't buy you another one? Give me a break."

"No, he didn't even want to buy me this one. He thinks my visions are bullshit."

I smirked at him, knowing full well no one would ever change his mind about his visions. "Maybe they are."

Trevor waved me off and moved on to better subjects to catch on camera. He seemed to focus on the sexy stuff, like Sam's roommate, who was still sucking face. She hadn't come up for air in about five minutes. She should've entered some kind of contest.

"Hey, do you want to dance?" Sam asked over the music. "One of the other dorms is strictly 'dancing only,' and Trevor is too busy with his documentary."

I would've said no; I should've. But she was giving those eyes that said, "If you say no, you might as well go home now." I was in no mood to argue with her tonight, considering I was halfway through a second cup. Dancing *could* be fun. We hadn't done it in years. Plus, we could dance together instead of her dancing with a boyfriend.

"Sure," I agreed, finishing my drink.

Just hours ago, I'd broken up with Eli, and now I was partying with college students at a school I didn't even go to. Was this how it would be from now on? Would I always feel like the weight had been lifted from my shoulders? I wasn't thinking about what my parents would do if they caught me out late. I didn't have to think about the judgemental looks Eli would give me either.

We were dancing, actually *dancing*. I didn't know what my feet were doing or where they were going, but they moved like I'd never seen them. Sam was next to me, laughing. She was enjoying watching me enjoy myself. She might have annoyed me with her attitude and life choices sometimes, but she was my only real, touchable, huggable friend. She wanted me to have fun and enjoy life.

She knew about my parents, but we didn't talk about them. She knew that I never let loose, couldn't unwind. This was her way of letting me do that. I'd noticed over time that when we did things like this, she kept an eye on me so I could get crazier than her.

"You got moves," a deep voice behind me shouted.

I whipped around so quickly my hair slapped the guy in the chest. He looked like he might be a basketball player. Blond hair, blue eyes. Typical. He was at least six feet tall, while I stood five foot four. He was lanky, but in a good way. He was wearing a tight green Polo that showed off his pecs and biceps.

"Thank you," I shouted, feeling my face getting hot. "Do you go to school here?"

What was I doing? Was I entertaining this guy?

"Nah, I got invited by Sam. She said her boyfriend was doing a movie. She's very convincing."

I scoffed. Of course Sam had invited him. She invited everyone to hit on me. I shouldn't care. It didn't matter anymore. There was no one I had to explain myself to; I could do whatever I wanted. I kept forgetting that.

"Do you have a name?" he asked, taking a step toward me.

"Do you?" I retorted.

"Matt."

"Eleanor."

Matt shook my hand and wouldn't let go. We just kept shaking. He laughed. "I'm sorry; I just have a feeling that if I let go, you're going to walk away from me."

I smirked, stopped shaking, and just held his hand in mine. "Am I that transparent?"

"You look uninterested. Which is OK. I'm a dumb jock and you look too smart for me."

"We're not in high school."

"High school never ends. Or so I've been told."

I hung around with Matt for a while longer. He told me about his sister and how she had mental deficits. He did in fact play basketball, and he'd started a charity for his sister to get her the help his family couldn't always afford. It was impressive. It was also a huge line to talk to girls he'd just met.

We had moved from the dancing room to a room at the end of the hall with jazz playing. It seemed strange to me that it was almost empty. There were a couple friends smoking pot in the corner. What kind of college was this? I couldn't believe every night could be like this.

I told him about what I'm studying— I decided to major literature and minor in history. It always interested me, but I never thought I'd have a chance study something at all. The teachers I had are hard; I knew that it would only benefit me, but they gave me a run for my money. I shouldn't have even been out right now.

"So." Here came the dreaded question. "Do you have a family?"

"No, I don't," I said flatly. "They died when I was little."

"Oh, so you were in the system with Sam? That explains how you know her."

"Sure," I said.

Matt stared at me with this look in his eyes like he was trying to figure me out. Maybe I was not doing the whole "have fun" thing right. Sam would scorn me for not having made out with him yet: "You're not trying to get to know these people. You're just having fun." Matt knew how to have fun but I didn't.

"You're different," he said. "You're reserved. You don't give a lot away."

It didn't sound like a compliment, but it also wasn't an insult. My cheeks were pink. I felt like someone was giving me surgery—like my body was open on a table and Matt was looking inside to find my secrets. I felt vulnerable, and I didn't like it. Eli had done this to me too, and I couldn't stand it.

"I like it," Matt stated.

"Thanks?"

"It's kind of nice. You don't trust people easily, and that's honestly a good thing."

Grabbing my hand, he pulled me in closer. He didn't smell like alcohol or pot. He smelled like he was sober. I liked *that*. Matt was going to kiss me. I could tell from the way he was looking at me. He rested his hand on my shoulder, gently pulling me closer.

"Eleanor," Sam shouted from behind. Her tear-soaked face told me something had happened. "I need you."

I sighed. "I'm sorry."

As I got up, Matt did too. He didn't ask for my phone number, he didn't stop me from walking toward Sam to see what was wrong. *Really* impressive. I gestured for Sam to give me one minute. She sighed and nodded, waiting at the door. I turned around and gathered enough courage to steal a simple kiss from Matt. He lingered, trying to draw it out, but I didn't have time. Sam was not patient.

"Don't leave yet," I whispered on his lips.

He chuckled. "I wouldn't dare."

* * *

Sam's dramatics made me sober up quicker than I wanted to. She kicked everyone out of her dorm, including her own roommate, who was less than thrilled.

"Trevor is such a douche!" Sam screeched. "He seriously wanted me to have *sex* with another girl on film. No. Like, I'll do a lot but not that. That's one hundred percent a porno, isn't it?"

She walked back and forth in the tiny space while I sat on the bed wondering how long was too long. Matt wouldn't wait forever, and I wanted to at least give him my phone number. He seemed like someone I could get to know.

"Are you even listening to me, Eleanor?"

I wasn't. I was thinking of someone else entirely. Sam went on to muse that "maybe it wouldn't be so bad, I would just have to forget about the camera," at which point I decided to leave her and make my way back to Matt. Just as he was walking from the jazz room, I caught him.

He was shaking his head and rubbing the back of his neck, like his ego had been bruised from waiting too long.

"Matt," I called, hoping he'd hear me through the crowded halls. I wondered why people were still up and about. I wished I was in bed. "Wait up."

"Eleanor. I was starting to get worried." Matt's face told me that he had hoped my friend really was having a "crisis" and I hadn't blown him off.

I smirked. "You know, from where I was standing, you looked like you were going to leave."

Matt laughed out loud, making me think of Eli and how he loved my sense of humor. "I don't leave."

* * *

Weeks went by, months. Matt and I were still getting to know each other; we told each other it wasn't serious, that we could quit anytime. I told him I'd just got out of a complicated relationship that didn't end well. I wasn't looking to do that again. I wanted something simple.

We were sitting in Central Park one afternoon with Sam and Trevor. Yes, they were still dating. No, Sam hadn't done the video. Trevor had found someone else to do it, which caused completely different complications. Matt sat with his back against a tree, and I was sitting between his legs, soaking in the sun. Trevor had a new vision: modern life in time lapse. His camera was recording us the whole time.

"So, like," Sam started. "You guys are together but not together?"

I nodded, and Matt said, "Yes."

"How does that even work?"

I snorted. "It just does for us. Doesn't mean it's for everybody."

"Are you only seeing each other?" Sam asked.

I shifted uncomfortably in Matt's arms. We hadn't talked about it. I wasn't seeing anyone else, but Matt had never said anything to the contrary. It was fine; I didn't want him to feel like this was just us. That would be a relationship. Something I didn't want.

Matt said, "*I* am. But we're not forcing that on each other, either."

I smiled to myself, thinking maybe something could come from nothing. Or it would stay nothing. I was OK with that too.

My phone pinged in my purse. I pulled it out to make sure no one at work needed a shift covered. It was almost spring break, and I was going to try to earn as much money over the course of a week as I could. My finances were becoming tighter as school went on.

It was Eli.

Eli had been emailing me once a month, keeping me in the loop. He hadn't dated; he was still waiting. School was harsh, but he was getting through it.

My face went slack and pale. I felt sick. No amount of time would ever heal the wound between us. I put my phone away quickly so Matt wouldn't notice, praying he also didn't notice my expression. I could tell my body language had changed; he held me differently.

"You know, I'm actually not feeling great all of a sudden," I said. I turned around to look at Matt, to see if he could tell I wasn't OK. "You ready to go?"

Matt looked worried, like I was acting strange and making up an excuse. Which was true. The sun was making the back of my neck sweat uncontrollably. I wanted to wrap myself in blankets on my couch, preferably alone. I didn't want to have to lie to Matt, to tell him it was a stomach bug.

"Yeah," Matt stated. "I'm getting pretty beat by this sun."

We walked to my apartment in silence, the kind you dread. Matt held my hand a little too tight, like he didn't want to let me go. My initial thought was that he had seen the email. He knew that I had previously been seeing someone else, and maybe he thought I still was. Maybe he thought this was over.

The apartment kept getting closer. My hands started to sweat. Matt stopped me.

"Are you really not feeling well?" he asked.

"Um, not really," I said. "I haven't eaten today. Maybe that's it."

This was what I'd been trying to avoid. That was why I'd been so quiet. Matt and I never ran out of things to talk about. Now I knew there was nothing I could say without lying to him, and I didn't want to. I was sick of lying to everyone around me. Especially about Eli. Matt looked at me like he was trying to figure me out.

"Do you want me to make you anything, just hang out?" He grabbed my sweaty hands, kissing one.

I didn't let go, but I dismissed his suggestion. "I think I'm just going to take a nap."

"OK."

Matt kissed me goodbye, and I went up to my apartment. My kitten, Tubbs, was waiting for me on the couch. He looked up from his lazy position, blinked, and laid his head back down. Uninterested, per usual. I was clutching my phone in my hand, feeling like if I let it go, everything that I'd worked so hard for would disappear. I was just starting to let him go and move on.

I read the email and reread the email. I spent the rest of the afternoon trying to read between the lines. I made dinner for myself and watched TV while reading the email again. Tubbs rubbed against my legs for food, which I gave him. I showered, cleaned my apartment. I avoided Matt's calls while I gave all my attention to that damn email.

I tossed and turned in bed, wearing the matching pajamas that Matt had bought me for Christmas. They were pink with donuts and sparkles. I hated sparkles but loved donuts. When he got it for me, it was unexpected. I hadn't thought we were there yet. He seemed to pay for every date, every meal. I hadn't got him a Christmas gift. I felt so bad that I went out the next day and got him the same thing.

"Now we can match," I said as I watched him put the sparkly jammies over his clothes.

"This is perfect," he said, grinning.

My life was finally normal. I felt normal. Matt, Sam, college, even my cat. I felt like I was making something for myself. I could have a life with someone and even start a family. That was a lifetime away, but it could happen. I *could* have that. I couldn't if I let Eli come back into my life. That had been the problem the first time.

Closing my eyes and taking a deep breath, I read the message one last time. I analyzed it again and then deleted it. And deciding that deleting it wasn't enough, I deleted all past emails as well. It helped, but it still wasn't enough. My mind was made up, and it wasn't going to change. Eli needed to be erased for good. Or at least, I needed to not exist in his life anymore. The only thing left to do was delete my email address.

After I did, a weight lifted from my chest. I felt like I could breathe. I felt like I could look Matt in the eyes and be honest with him about things now. Mostly.

Tubbs meowed, climbing into bed with me. I finally mustered the courage to call Matt, praying silently that he wouldn't be mad at me for ignoring him all afternoon. The phone rang and rang. When I thought about giving up, I heard Matt on the other end.

"Hey, Eleanor," he mumbled, like he'd just woken up.

"Hey," I said. "I'm sorry if I woke you."

"It's OK." There was a pause. He was mad. "What's up?"

"I just—" My turn to pause as I tried to come up with a good excuse for not answering him. "I've been thinking about us a lot."

"Oh?" Matt shuffled on the other end, most likely sitting up to prepare for my words.

"Yeah. Sam and Trevor made me think more and—"

"If you're breaking up with me, you don't have to say anything. I kind of got that vibe today."

"What? No. Matt, I want the opposite." He didn't say anything, so I continued. "I was thinking about what they said, and I would actually like more. I wouldn't mind if you were my boyfriend."

"Oh, really?" I could hear the smile in his voice. "That wouldn't be so bad."

Feeling myself smile, I told him I liked the idea. We talked the rest of the night and fell asleep on the phone together. I promised myself I wouldn't let my past get in the way of my future. I promised myself that no matter what happened from this point on, it wouldn't be because of Eli. I could love someone. I could be with someone, and it could be *real*.

Eli

Age 22

Eleanor stood in front of me. Words were coming out of her mouth, but I couldn't seem to hear them. Everything was muted, muddled. The last thing I'd heard her say was that she wouldn't be able to see me as much. That her life was becoming too hectic, and I was distracting her.

"I can't pretend I don't have things going on. For the first time ever, I feel like things are going right for me. I feel good. *Free.*"

I scoffed at her, crossing my arms. "For the first time *ever*? Really?"

"Yes, Eli. Ever," she deadpanned. "What's your problem?"

"You're becoming my problem!" I said angrily. I walked away, wishing I didn't have to yell at her.

There had never been a time that Eleanor wasn't with me. In this life, in my real life. I couldn't do this. I couldn't live without her. She was too much to let go of. I felt sick. I *felt* sick. I had never felt anything here. It made me afraid I was starting to wake up, and I couldn't let this be my last memory with her. I pushed down the bile in my throat and looked back at her.

She looked helpless, like this wasn't easy on her either. Like nothing I could say would change anything. I made my way back to her. I grabbed her face in my hands and pressed my lips to hers. Like always, she tried to push me off, but it didn't take long before she melted in my arms. She wanted this as much as I did; in the end it was always going to be just us.

I bit her lip, and she moaned, her hips pressed against me. We were still standing, but my knees were weak. Eleanor grabbed my arms like she needed something to hold on to. Then she pushed me away.

"What the hell, Eli?" she shouted, wiping her mouth. "Why do you have to do that? I'm...I'm not OK with that anymore."

My heart was still pounding in my chest, and I was still trying to control my breathing. "What do you mean? Why are you telling me any of this?"

El looked me in the eye. "We need to move on. *I* need to move on."

I gaped at her. "Move on? *Move on?* Why would you want to move on? Is there someone else?"

"No. God, Eli..." She bit her lip. "But there could be."

"You want to be with someone else. Find someone else."

"I have a few times. This," Eleanor gestured to the space between us and around us, "this is making things impossible. I can't move on and be with someone else if you're still in my life. You can't either."

"I don't *want* to, love. I thought that this was us, forever," I said, trying to keep my voice even. I could feel my throat start to clog with regret and tears. "I've offered to come be with you. I've offered to bring you to me."

"Don't you see how fucked up that is?" She sighed. "We don't know what kind of life we could have without each other. It's always been Eli and Eleanor. We've never tried to live a life alone.

"And you paying for me to come to a place I don't know just seems selfish. And I can't make you come to me. You're in medical school. You can't do that. You'd probably have to start over, or worse, not start again at all. You'd resent me, or I would resent you. We'd hate each other. I'm not doing that. I won't."

There was no changing her mind. What Eleanor wanted from me, she got. She deserved that much. I couldn't argue with her, and I didn't want to. I couldn't imagine a life without her, but if I kept pushing the subject, she wouldn't want to see me at all.

"OK," I said, clearing my throat. "OK."

"OK?" Eleanor echoed, walking closer to me. "I won't be gone completely. I just. We can't anymore. I need to grow up, and I need to grow alone. Find out who I can be by myself, you know?"

"You'll still contact me? You'll still want to see me?"

"I always want to see you, Eli. Always."

I told her I loved her, and she said it back. In all the times we'd see each other, all the times I'd whispered it when we were kissing, making love, just walking around in Crystal Palace Park, never once had she said it back.

Was it a sign for hope? Would she come back to me one day? My life didn't work without her, and she knew that. She knew I needed her. I wouldn't survive my father, my friends. I couldn't do it without her as my backbone.

We spent the rest of the dream together. It seemed like hours. For the first time in a long time, we had no interruptions until my alarm went off, pulling me away from her. She told me she loved me again, she told me we would see each other again, before she disappeared.

* * *

After that dream, there were many nights when I woke in a cold sweat, *almost there*. Almost in our world. I could feel her breath on my face and hear her saying "I love you" over and over. Sometimes I tried so hard it hurt. My brain wouldn't allow it when there was no one on the other end wanting me back.

Weeks went by, months. I told myself she was busy making a life for herself. I told myself she was still coming back to me. I emailed her once a month to update her on my life. I let her know how school was going, and I told her how much I missed her. I was ready for her to come back.

* * *

Six months it had been. I'd given up emailing a long time ago, but to-day, I was feeling optimistic. I opened my laptop, which was supposed to be for work only, per my father. I bookmarked the inbox used only for Eleanor. I didn't say much. I let her know she was missed.

Hey El. I hope you're doing well.

I honestly haven't been doing great. School has been killing me and so has my father. He's always lurking over my shoul-der, waiting for me to screw up so he can tell me how badly I suck. Lol.

Anyway, I miss you.

I hit send without a subject line and started working on my school-ing. Becoming a surgeon was not something I took lightly, and my workload was not light either. I felt as though I carried a weight on each shoulder and my back. My dad sat on the left shoulder, the weak-er one. He told me what a horrible doctor I'd be if I didn't study. He told me I would never be as good as he was. How disappointed he'd always be.

My right shoulder, that was just the schoolwork. The stack of books rose higher than my head. I had pencils and paper scratching my neck, waiting to be used.

My back. On my back was Eleanor and everything she stood for. Even if my shoulders were free, Eleanor made it hard to walk. She sat on my back telling me she loved me. She laughed at the things I laughed at, and she made sure I knew that she would never leave my side, no matter how much I begged.

My laptop *ping*ed, letting me know I had an email. It was not my school email. My hands were shaking as I clicked. I told myself this time was different. This time, she'd answer, and this time she'd want to see me. I wouldn't overstep or ask too many questions. I would be rational and calm.

I was greeted with two short sentences:

We're sorry, the email address you have tried to contact is either no longer in use or it was not inputted correctly. Please check the email you have provided or try again later.

Eli

Present Day

The air is brisk today, but the sun is shining through the clouds. I have my sunglasses on, but the sun is just as bright. Austin skips beside me, jumping in every puddle he can find. And if I tell him not to, it only makes him want to do it more. Eleanor is wearing gloves, her chipped blue-polished fingertips sticking out the ends. She has hot chocolate in her hands. She keeps it close to her face for warmth.

It's winter in New York, something I'm not used to. December seems to have brought the cold front Eleanor warned me about. I keep my hands in my pockets because I didn't bring any gloves. I didn't think I'd need them.

"The library isn't much farther," El says. She hands me her cup, her face full of mockery. "Do you need to keep your hands warm?"

I scoffed. "If I take my hands out of my pockets, I'll lose my fingers, love."

She laughs and nudges me playfully.

Traveling with Eleanor is a great experience. My time getting to know Austin is something I'll treasure for the rest of my life. There are times I have to remind myself he isn't my son. That he doesn't belong to me, no matter how much I want him to.

Grudgingly, Lana trudges behind us. Eleanor refused to leave London without her, and since then, she's come and gone as she pleases. She always comes back, though. She never comes back drunk, never questions my motives. I knew that Austin might have a problem with me coming into the picture, but Lana was unexpected.

"Hey gorgeous," Lana calls, "are we almost there?"

"I think so."

El sighs. Lana won't talk to her. She seems to accept the fact that I'm around, but she doesn't want to be the first to say sorry. She doesn't want anyone to tell her "forget about James," even though no one is asking her to.

"Have you talked to John lately?" Eleanor asks, grabbing my arm.

"Yes, actually, about a week ago."

John called a month back to let me know he's going to be a father. Willow's having morning sickness pretty bad. At first they weren't sure why. When they finally went to the doctor, she found out she was pregnant. It's only been three months, but they're so excited. When he called, John was freaking out.

"I can't be a dad yet!" he said. "I'm still such a wanker."

"You'll be a great father, John." I told him. "You'll be a responsible wanker."

When I told Eleanor, she immediately asked for Willow's number so she could give her tips and tricks. "Every woman should try these things. It'll help. I'd be doing a disservice if I didn't tell her." I didn't argue, and they've been friends since.

"They went for their four-month checkup. John Jr. is doing fantastic."

"You don't even know if it's a boy!" Eleanor gripes. "They're waiting to find out the gender."

"I know, I'm just hopeful. I'd love to have a little nephew."

"You already have Austin."

I smile at El. "I'm really hoping he won't be my nephew, love."

She blushes and drops the subject. We've talked so much about being *together*. The words "I love you" have been thrown around more times than I can count. We *love* each other. But nothing is official. Nothing is made into words. I'm OK with that for now. Eleanor is back in my life, and I can't ask for more.

She doesn't know it yet, but I've been planning to marry her since I decided to go on this trip with her. I've dropped hints now and again, and she doesn't object to them. Sometimes, she gets excited, thinking it will happen soon, which gives me hope that there will be a "yes" in the near future. There's one little boy I need approval from first.

We get to the library, and Eleanor goes inside with Lana. A lot of the time, I take Austin to do tourist things while El has her book readings. Today, Austin has decided to show me around his home city. He's six now, he knows everything, and he definitely does not need a babysitter.

"Do you want to go to the apartment?" Austin exclaims, jumping up and down.

Taking the subway to the apartment is exciting all on its own. Austin doesn't sit down for a second, but he makes it very clear he has to pee. The stop is just a block from the front door, and we run the whole way there.

There's a cat meowing at the door as Austin unlocks it. Tubbs. He's not a normal cat. Tubbs makes faces at you like he knows what you're saying, and he doesn't care what you want or don't want; he does what *he* wants. He's fat and old, on death's doorstep. "Best to just not bother him," Eleanor says.

Austin comes out of the bathroom, sighing. "That feels good!"

As we go around the apartment, he shows me all his things—the toys he's currently fascinated by and the kitchenware specifically for him. "Momma says I'm going to grow out of this stuff, but I don't see how." I laugh at how honest she was, as much as I'm not surprised.

Entering Austin's room, I can't imagine him growing up anywhere else. It looks like El painted the walls for him. There are clouds on the ceiling and walls, and the carpet looks like the sky as well. As a kid, I would've loved this. Falling asleep with the clouds above me like I was flying…

"Did your mother do this?" I ask.

Austin shakes his head no. "My dad did." He shrugs. "It's been like this since I was born."

"Oh, well, he did a very good job."

I sit down on Austin's airplane-shaped bed, wincing when it creaks. He has a nightstand that looks like a pilot. Sitting on top is the same picture Eleanor keeps on her bedside table. James was never not smiling, it seems. All the pictures I've ever seen of him, he's the light.

"Hey lad, come sit next to me." I pat the spot next to me, hoping Austin isn't in a playful mood. When he sits down next to me, I sigh inwardly with relief. "Now, you know I love your mum, right?"

Austin nods. "I think so. You make good pancakes."

I chuckle. "Yeah, I guess I do. Well, I wanted to ask you something. I've been waiting a while to do this, maybe I'm just scared, but you know, I think it's enough waiting." Austin looks at me like I'm crazy, like he couldn't care less. "I know that I could never replace your father, and I don't want to. He gave you life, and I didn't."

Austin ducks his head like he's thinking hard about what I'm saying. I know how hard it must be for him to understand, as young as he is. Something like this probably doesn't make sense. He starts to cry.

"But I would really love to be in your life for the rest of mine. You have made such an impact on me, and I can only think it's for a reason. Not only have I fallen in love with your mother, I've fallen in love with you, Austin. You are *so* important to me."

He's now hiccupping, making it difficult to finish. I get down on my knees in front of him with his hands in mine. Eleanor would tell me I'm ruining my luxurious pants. "Austin, will you be my stepson?"

"Yes!" Austin is in my arms in a second, crying and giggling. "I love you, Eli."

"I love you, lad."

The rest of the hour, we stay in his bedroom while I tell him all about my plan to propose to Eleanor. He gives me some good ideas. One includes a hot air balloon. "That's a good one too, but I don't think I could find one on such short notice," I tell him, and he thinks some more. Tonight will be the night, and I'll make sure Austin is there to watch it happen.

* * *

"So where are we going?" Eleanor asks, wrapping her scarf tighter around her neck.

It's colder now than it was during the day. There's no sun to give us any warmth at all. I tell myself this was a good idea and I have to stick with it. I'm just as cold as she is, and I have less on.

"You know this city better than I do, love. You tell me."

El sighs. "I know where, but you're supposed to tell me anyway."

Laughing, I lead her through Central Park. We walk for a little while, until all of a sudden—

"Oh my god," Eleanor whispers. "Is that—"

"Is it what?" I ask, playfully.

In the middle of the park is a mattress. It's as soft as any I could dream of. Austin helped me pick it out. The park is mostly empty because of the cold, so it hasn't been too difficult to keep people away from everything I set up. I drag a starstruck Eleanor toward the mattress. We sit down, and she closes her eyes.

"God, it seems like it was only yesterday sometimes."

"I'm glad it wasn't," I tell her, lying down. "We've both changed so much. It took a lot to get to this point."

Eleanor lies down next to me. Her eyes are suspicious. "That's true. What *aren't* you saying right now?"

I wink. "You know, my parents. They used to get me the coolest toys ever. I had so many. I was spoiled rotten."

She laughs. "I was jealous."

Behind her, I now see Lana helping Austin lug a giant teddy bear onto a boulder. Austin's breath huffs in the air as he pushes it to sit up straight. He hides behind it while Lana climbs down and crouches out of sight. Even she has accepted this. She knows I'm a decent person, as much as she'd prefer James.

I nod in the direction of the teddy bear. When Eleanor looks, she gasps. "What the hell are you doing?"

"Why don't we go over and find out?"

I can only imagine how weak Eleanor's legs are feeling, because I'm having trouble walking over to the bear myself. I've done this once—proposed. I thought there wasn't a chance in hell that Kit would say no. But she did. It was devastating. Putting myself out there again, doing this again, terrifies me.

It was always meant to be Eleanor. Even when I loved Kit, Eleanor had my heart. She was in every memory, every dream. Everything I ever wanted was her, and I never could see my life a different way. That's changed. Everything I wanted before is different now. The future I planned for us isn't the future I've been given. This one is better.

"You know, from the day I met you, I knew you were special. I knew there was something about this girl that made her different from the girls in my classes. You made me feel butterflies. You made me tingly. I remember wishing I didn't have to wake up.

"You helped me get through so many things, and you didn't even know it. Maybe it was unconventional. Maybe I didn't always tell you. But you went through so much that nothing in my life seemed so bad. I guess that sounds awful, but it shouldn't. You helped me get through the harder things, because in my head, I always thought 'It could be worse,' and it could've been."

The lump in my throat is starting to choke me. I help Eleanor onto the boulder. Her eyes look glassy as I meet her at the top. She's trying very hard to hold back tears as she stares at the bear. It has a ribbon around its neck with a ring hanging from it. She turns to me, now patiently waiting to hear what I have to say.

"Eleanor, I want you to be the one to help me get through everything else. I want you to be there to remind me that it could always be worse. I've known I wanted to spend the rest of my life with you since the moment I met you. You showed me that I could never be too grateful for what I had.

"Tonight, I wanted to show you how grateful I am. You deserve more than a ring and a long speech, but I am only good at so much. So, there's only one thing left to do."

Austin emerges from behind the bear and I get down on one shaky knee. Eleanor exclaims, clapping. She's sniffling, smiling, wiping tears from her eyes. She grabs Austin to stand with her, but he tugs away from her to grab the ring off the bear. Then he comes to stand next to me, something she wasn't expecting.

"Will you marry him?" he asks.

"Will you marry me?" I ask. Holding El's hand, I fight back tears and wait for an answer.

"Yes," Eleanor says.

A small crowd has formed, along with the photographer I hired and Lana. They're all clapping and cheering.

Austin slides the ring onto his mother's ring finger. He jumps into her arms, kissing her cheek. "I love you, Momma," he says, holding her tight. I stand up, my legs no longer shaking. They're so numb from the cold that they can't feel anything else.

Eleanor pulls me close, the heat from her cheeks radiating onto mine. She kisses me, still holding Austin. He gags and wriggles free, running to the bear. The deal we made was that if he helped me pull this off, if his mother said yes, he could keep the bear.

This kiss starts to thaw me out. This kiss makes all the other kisses we've ever shared seem like light work. This kiss means the beginning of the rest of our lives together. This kiss means that we'll be there for each other through everything, no matter what we're thinking or feeling. This kiss means we won't have to worry anymore about one of us disappearing.

This kiss is a promise.

Eleanor

Present Day

My left hand feels heavy, weighed down by the giant rock hanging from my ring finger. Diamonds twist down the side of the band. The diamond in the center is round, surrounded by more tiny diamonds. It must've cost Eli more than a few months' rent. I can't believe it's on *my* finger.

Uncertainty about the future lingers in the back of my mind. It never really goes away. But now, it isn't as loud. My mind is more focused on color schemes and how quickly we can get married. I don't want to wait a moment longer.

The last few months have changed so many things. I was so scared to let Eli in again, terrified that if I did, I would lose not only him but myself. It took so long to be who I needed to be again. It wasn't just the fear that things wouldn't work. My first husband *died*. How could I just jump right back into trusting that it wouldn't happen again?

Eli made it seem so simple. Everything for him was easy and carefree. Up until now, I didn't know how to be the way he was. I was always thinking about the worst possible outcomes instead of the good ones that were just as possible. All the times I pushed him away and he kept coming back—it was all because he knew we could have something special. He knew this was real.

"Momma, do I get to be in the wedding?" Austin asks one morning while I pour him his cup of milk.

We've just finished breakfast. He had a couple frozen waffles, and I had a bagel. Eli is at his hotel this morning, officially checking out.

He'll have to go back to London at some point to get the rest of his affairs in order, but he wants to be with us for a while. We've already decided where we'll live. He wants to be wherever we are, and we're in Manhattan. That was something I needed figured out as soon as possible, for Austin's sake and mine as well.

"Of course, baby." I hand him the cup. "What do you want to be?"

"Can I hold the rings?"

"Do you think you'll be able to? You have to make sure you don't lose them."

Austin's eyes go wide, like it's a big responsibility. "I think I can handle it."

We sit and talk about what rings we want to get. My dress should be in tomorrow. So will Sam. Eli isn't thrilled, but he knows she's my only other friend. He'll finally get to meet her, and maybe things will be different. Lana got a dress and asked if there'll be an open bar. Though there won't, she's still coming.

When Eli gets to the apartment, his arms are full of boxes. Austin sees him and offers to help him carry them. He hobbles to my—*our*—bedroom, grunting softly when he sets the heavy box down.

"That was nice of him," Eli says, joining me on the couch.

"Did you get everything figured out?" I ask.

He waves his hand and says, "Not really. That's OK, though, we will."

Anxiety creeps up my back. My mind runs wild over the future issues we might run into. Eli probably hasn't even called his family yet. I know I'm being crazy—it hasn't even been twenty-four hours since he proposed—but I can't help it. This is what I do when I feel like things are spinning out of control.

"Hey, love," Eli says, pulling me from my downward spiral. "Don't do that. I can literally hear you worrying."

I smirk. "Yeah, well, you know me…"

"I do. And I know you can't control everything. So, let the chips fall. Loosen your shoulders. We will get this all taken care of, I promise you."

As he rubs my shoulders, I feel myself start to melt. Eli's promise feels like the first of many to come. It feels like I can believe him. The promises he makes never waver; they never make me feel like I'm being blown off. He kisses my forehead and I know. I know that this is the only promise I need.

* * *

White surrounds me and Lana, overwhelming us with frills and lace. I take a breath, hoping, praying that this day will go by as quickly as possible. The dress arrived later than expected. Over a week. The wedding shop called this morning, letting me know it was ready for fitting.

Here I am with Lana, waiting for the shopgirl to bring my dress out. I twirl my ring around on my finger, an annoying habit I picked up quickly. All at once I'm bear-hugged by a four-foot-eight-inch brat squealing at the top of her lungs. Sam draws judging looks from every employee in the store but doesn't seem to care. Neither does Lana as she sits in a chair waiting for this day to be over.

"Oh my god, you're getting married!" Sam jumps up and down, jewelry jingling. "Well, again."

Sam has remarried four times. Either her husbands cheated on her or she cheated on them, but none of them ever signed a prenup, so Sam was more than happy to take their money with her. She now lives on the Upper East Side in a mansion of an apartment with her teenage daughter. The first man she married solely because she got pregnant. She didn't mind either, because he had money.

Needless to say, Sam doesn't judge me for getting married again.

"God, I'm excited. I can't wait to meet Eli finally." She glances at Lana and whispers, "Do you remember when you told me about him? I can't believe you're marrying him!"

"I know, it's insane. Imagine how I'm feeling."

The employee helping me, Tanya, brings my dress out. Sam squeals again, pulling me toward it. Lana reluctantly follows. The ring-twirling picks up again, and I can feel my face getting warm. Sweat trickles down my back, making me wish I didn't have to do this today. I'd rather have a dress too big for me.

"Alright, so you can change in the room. Come out and let us know what you think!"

As I'm changing, I hear Sam say, in her nicest voice, "Tanya, is there any way we can get champagne over here right away?"

Lana agrees. I laugh to myself, not surprised that they hit it off.

The dress fits great. It's strange, wearing another dress. The first one was so different. It still hangs in the back of my closet. This one has sequins down to my hips, trailing off further down, and it hugs my curves in the right places and has a train a mile long. The spaghetti straps fall off the sides, hanging on my arms right where I want them.

When I come out of the dressing room, Sam and Lana are pouring themselves champagne. Sam fills her glass halfway, while Lana fills hers until it almost spills over. They both hold back laughter. When they notice me watching them, their expressions change.

Sam, dramatic as always, gasps out loud. She stands up, setting down her untouched drink. "You look *gorgeous*," she tells me. She hugs me, and I can hear her sniffling. Soon, I feel like I can't breathe with her holding me so tightly. I let go, and she does too.

Lana is still sipping her drink, smiling at me lightly. "You do look beautiful."

"Thank you."

"I'm glad I got to be here to see this one. I know I was off galivanting when you did your first fitting for James."

I shrug. "It happens."

Lana chuckles. I stand in front of the full-length mirror, staring at myself. This is *really* happening. I'm marrying the man of my dreams, and no one will ever know how literally. I can't believe it. Waking up next to Eli every morning makes me pinch myself. And it hurts like hell, so it has to be real.

For a split second, I almost wish my mother was here. It's brief, but it's there. Even after the therapy, after they changed, I can't wrap my head around having a close relationship with them. No one ever wants to bury their parents, but burying a husband on top of that makes it that much harder. I didn't have James with me to bury them. I didn't have him there to bury *himself*. He was gone.

All my life, I wished my parents would just die. I don't deny it; what they did to me as a child was so despicable that I couldn't think of anything else. I was so scared of them that any other ending seemed impossible.

Now that my mom is actually gone, I think having her with me would make this easier. Not because I need her, but because she was my mom. Once things were "fixed" and I started warming to the idea of having my parents around, I thought of the future. I never could imagine them being close with Austin, it didn't seem like something that I would ever be able to let go of. But us, we could've started over.

I start to twist my ring. I can't lose Eli. I can't do that again. I can't put Austin through that again. This time he'd remember; he wouldn't forget Eli like he forgot James. He knows who his father was, but he never got to *know* him. Austin already loves Eli and knows that Eli loves him. What if he leaves too?

Almost as if he knows I'm thinking about him, Eli calls while I'm still staring at myself with the dress on.

"Hey," I say, sighing.

"Hey, love," Eli pauses. I can hear the TV in the background. "You're not getting cold feet now, are you?"

"What's cold feet?" Austin shouts. I can imagine him lying on his belly too close to the television.

"It's what happens when you try on your wedding dress: no socks," Eli jokes. Austin laughs, and I can hear Eli finding somewhere quieter to talk. I go back into the dressing room. The girls give me suspicious looks. "Really, El. You all right?"

I clear my throat. There's a lump forming that I didn't notice until now. "I'm fine. It's not cold feet, I promise…" I hold my breath. "I just don't want to lose you. I know things can't possibly happen the same way, but really, I don't *know* that. It freaks me out."

"Yeah, well, I guess that's life, right?"

"What do you mean?"

Eli starts chuckling. "Well, you really never know what's going to happen. No one does. I think you and I are prime examples of that."

"Yeah…"

"'Never let the fear of striking out keep you from playing the game.' Babe Ruth."

Just like that, the anxiety is gone. I won't ever know what's going to happen, and I know that if roles were reversed, Eli wouldn't hesitate to be with me for the rest of our lives. He just lost his father, but it hasn't changed how he feels for me or how he wants to live *his* life. He knows that no matter what, he wants me to be there.

"I didn't realize you were such a baseball fan," I joke. My heart rate slows. I sit in the dressing room composing myself, wishing anything that Eli was with me right now.

"I'm not, but I am a fan of you."

Church bells. For years, the sound of church bells brought me nothing but pain and sorrow. For once in my life, that isn't the case. I'm wearing white, not black. I'm nervous, but ready for the future. I can feel it. Today is going to be different. Today is going to change the rest of our lives. After today, I'll be married. After today, I'll have a husband. I'll wake up in bed with him and wonder how I got *here*.

After today, I'll know love again.

Everything up to this moment, as I stand beside Eli at the altar, is already a blur. I vaguely remember Lana making us all choke down a shot before walking down the aisle. I know I felt dread inside when my hair wouldn't stay curled, but it's long gone. I barely remember the deja-vu sense that I've done this before. I can't dredge up grief for the lost ones I laid to rest in this very church.

I know that Eli is with me now, looking into my eyes. I saw that same look when I was six years old, climbing a tree with ungodly strength. There's a spark in his eye that shows how well he knows me. He sees right through me—he always has.

"Eleanor, repeat after me…"

"Eli, I love you. You are my best friend. Today I give myself to you in marriage. I promise to encourage you and inspire you, to laugh with you, and to comfort you in times of sorrow and struggle. I promise to love you in good times and in bad. When life seems easy and when it seems hard. When our love is simple, and when it is an effort. I promise to cherish you and to always hold you in the highest regard.

"These things I give to you today, and all the days of my life."

Eli repeats after the preacher as well. I listen to every word carefully, and to the compassion in his voice as he makes his promises. Promises I believe with all my heart. I watch his eyes well up with tears as he stares back at me. Our hands are intertwined, and I hold on tighter. I never want this moment to end.

Time stands still. I feel like my head is spinning, my heart is racing. I feel like I'm being spun around with my eyes closed. Eli is standing in front of me, still smiling. But my vision blurs, my throat is in my stomach. Fear closes in around me. *What's happening?* My grip on Eli's hands is slipping. It feels like I'm falling down a rabbit hole. It feels like I'm dreaming.

Epilogue

Eleanor

Present Day

Gasping, she wakes in the dark. Her silky nightgown sticks to her back with sweat. She tries to catch her breath as her eyes adjust to the dark. She sees the digital clock across from her, screaming the time: 3:47 a.m. She can hear cars honking outside. New York City's nightlife is still charming as ever.

When she can finally see, she notices she's not alone in the queen-sized bed. There's a man next to her, snoring softly. James. She thinks to herself, *James is dead*. She pokes him, hoping he'll just poof out of the room like a figment of her imagination.

He groans and turns over to face her. It *is* James. How is this possible? He died when Austin was just a baby. Along with her parents, who she never imagined reconciling with. Eleanor runs her fingers through her hair and finds a ring on her finger. She's still married. She was just getting married again. This is the ring James gave her, the beautiful diamond twist band. Just what she wanted. Just what they could afford.

"What the hell?" Eleanor whispers as her hand covers her mouth.

She gets up to stretch legs that now feel like Jell-O. She knows if she can find something, any sign of Eli, then maybe, just maybe, it was real. Memories start flying through her head. They *are* memories. Everything feels so real. Eleanor finds her way into Austin's room. He's still asleep in his airplane bed. She can't help but wonder what her five year old son dreaming about. She wonders why she gave him an airplane bed.

Hands wrap around her waist. She nearly jumps out of her skin. It's James.

"Hey," he murmurs lazily into her hair. "You OK? You're feverish."

Eleanor realizes something she hasn't thought in over ten years: she's started dreaming again. Everything she thought was real—running into Eli in London, meeting his father in his last moments of life…the love. What's happened to the dates they went on before Eli proposed? What's happened to Eli?

She and Eli never had dreams where other people were involved. They never had family or friends in their dreams where they're completely made up. They never had enough strength to do something so in depth. Eleanor couldn't believe this was happening.

Nothing happening now feels real. James, with his arms wrapped around her, doesn't *feel* real. But she knows what's happening. All the reasons she left Eli behind, all the times she rejected him. *This* is why.

James never died. He's still here with her, kissing his way down her neck. Her legs feel like Jell-O for a different reason now, but she still can't seem to shake the feeling that something isn't right. James is clouding her judgement. Panic seeps in. She's scared she doesn't know what reality is anymore.

She's forgotten what her real life is like.

When she pulls away from James slightly, his body language changes. He's tense now as he holds her. Why is she so worked up? She's had dreams with Eli before; this one was just so vivid, so real. Never has she been in the Dreamworld for such a long time. It scares her. All the other dreams that they had seemed so far away now, all those memories together seemed like nothing compared to this one.

Her feelings for Eli, hidden away in a box in the back of her mind, are starting to seep through. That scares her too. For such a long time, she's made sure that box remained sealed; now, after all this time, she's feeling things she never wants to feel again. But Eli isn't here, and he doesn't want to be. He moved on and found a better life for himself. She knows that already. When he wakes up in the morning, he'll have forgotten all about the dream. He won't remember her at all.

She takes a deep breath, turning herself around to wrap her arms around her husband's neck, stare into his worried eyes, and whisper, "It was just a dream. Let's go back to bed."

Eli

Present Day

*E*li's forehead beads with sweat as he startles awake. His bare chest feels so tight he can hardly sit up in his bed. The duvet he's tangled up in is making him feel trapped. There's a woman sleeping soundly next to him in one of the silky pink gowns she knows he loves.

He looks at his phone to see the time. 7:47 a.m. His throat feels so dry he thinks he might throw up, so he eases out of bed, trying not to disturb the woman lying next to him. She stirs slightly, just enough for him to get a glimpse of the giant rock on her left hand. It looks so familiar to him. He's seen that ring before...

Was he dreaming? The back of his neck breaks out in a sweat. He needs to drink something. *Anything.* Preferably bourbon, neat. His pajama pants have little pink pigs on them, and he wonders how the joke came about. Has he forgotten the life he's living?

Eleanor. He hears her voice in his head saying "I do" while Austin James handed him the wedding band she'd wear forever. He can feel her lips on his still; his heart starts to race again just thinking about it.

He walks out of his bedroom. He's in a giant flat. The kitchen looks big enough to feed thousands, and the TV in the living room belongs in a movie theater. For a moment, he forgot he was a surgeon who could afford this luxurious life.

The fridge is stocked with anything he could ever want to drink. The freezer has what he really wants: vodka. He pulls the bottle out, and as it touches the warm air, the glass frosts. It's mesmerizing.

When he finally finds the glasses, he pours himself a shot. Choking it down, he looks around at his home one more time. His eyes make their way back to the bedroom. He watches his fiancée crawl out of bed and shuffle into the kitchen.

He has another flashback—his fiancée's blonde hair pulled back in a low bun, tears in her eyes, a smile on her face. Eli remembers reconnecting with her after the breakup, taking her out to dinner to explain the heartache and pain from his past. He remembers proposing again, her saying yes, wedding plans emailed to him everyday while he's working, the stress of everything that needs to be finished.

"Kit," he says, surprised he even remembers her name. Memories start to flood back. "Go back to bed, love."

Kit comes over to his side, resting her head on his bare shoulder. Her golden hair smells like apples, and memories of washing it for her when she was sick come back into his mind. How she stuck by him through everything, including his father's viciousness. She's strong enough to stand with him in his darkest moments.

"Did you have another dream about your father?" Kit asks, pouring him another shot. This has happened before. "It's been over a year, babe."

Eli's chest closes up at the memory of his father's last breaths. Kit was there with him then as well. The memory feels distorted. Eleanor was there too. He'll go mad trying to figure out what's real and what isn't. Maybe he could look her up…

He takes the shot.

Eleanor isn't here. She never has been and never will be. He knows what's happening, and he starts to remember who he is and who loves him. He thinks back to Don and his therapy. Eli loved Eleanor once, and the past will never change, but he let her go a long time ago.

Eli kisses Kit on the forehead and pulls her close. Her arms wrap around him tightly, and she sighs. Whether it's the alcohol in his blood or Kit's comforting embrace, he starts to feel warm and tired again. His eyes feel heavy, but as he closes them, the only person he can see is fiery hair and emerald eyes.

"It was just a dream, love," Eli says into Kit's hair. "It was just a dream."